SALTUS

CJ Hatton

First published 2022 by Chalk Road Press

ISBN: 9798842042937

Copyright CJ Hatton 2022

All rights reserved. No part of this publication may be reproduced or distributed in any form without prior written permission from the author, with the exception of non-commercial uses permitted by copyright law.

The right of CJ Hatton to be identified as the author of this work has been asserted by him in accordance with the Copyright, Design and Patents Act 1988

SALTUS

Saltus: /ˈsaltəs/ •n poetic/literary a sudden transition; a breach of continuity. ORIGIN C17: from L., lit. 'leap'.

For the days that stretch out ahead hold more sorrow than joy, and the body whose limbs once gave you pleasure will soon give you none, when you've lived past your prime. And when the Caregiver comes, he ends all lives the same way. Hades is suddenly real—no lyre, no dancing, no marriage-song. There is nothing but Death. By any measure, it is best never to have been born. But once a man is born, the next best thing, by far, is for him to return, as soon as he can, to the place he came from. For once youth—with its mindless indulgence—goes by, is there a single punishing blow that won't find him? Any misfortune that doesn't attack his life? Envy, feuding, revolt, battle, and murder! And finally, old age: despised, decrepit, lonely, friendless old age takes him in — there he keeps house with the worst of all evils.

Sophocles: Oedipus at Kolonos; Trans. Robert Bagg

Repository of Human Experience
Statement of Intent

The United Nations established the Repository of Human Experience (R.H.E.) in the year 2053. Housed in ground-stations around the globe, the R.H.E. will provide a deep-time post-extinction record of human accomplishment and knowledge for the benefit of the next intelligent species to evolve on or visit the earth. It is a vast undertaking and the work is ongoing.

The R.H.E. recognises and records the lives of many individuals. Its principal criteria for selection are achievement in a recognised field and uniqueness of experience. Millions more whose lives might otherwise pass unrecorded are selected by annual lottery.

Deposition 91GK637
I, Khristos (Kit) Zachariades, meet the second of these criteria.
 01:17:43 European Standard Time
 09-22-2091

This text is automatically converted from audio recordings. Ellipses indicate the removal of untranscribable content. Intentional breaks in the recording are indicated by Ω.

This process may be subject to minor errors.

Transcript 001

Unidentified human male: It is a strange business, this talking to myself. I do, of course, if only to break the silence, but I doubt it makes sense, what I say.

Acquiring voice profile.

My helpmate, Wendy, is so used to our routine I rarely need to instruct him, and even then, I'm not sure he's listening.

As for you, I'm speaking but you're not listening either.

Not yet anyway.

But introductions: I am Khristos Zachariades. Everyone calls me Kit.

Voice profile acquired. Khristos Zachariades, designated witness. Tagged as Kit.

Kit: An Englishman by birth and by father, I survive alone on an island in the Aegean. Greece was my mother's country. The summers are hot and the winters cold. My age, thank you for asking, is sixty-four years eight months and fourteen days. No doubt you are aware of the significance.

You are hearing me through a Com-Tech audio recorder and transmitter hanging round my neck. Never worn it before and it's lighter than I thought. Powered by my movement and uploads data to a passing satellite. Assuming there's any left. It also monitors my heartbeat. When that ceases it transmits the final recording and my name and location are entered in a virtual book of the dead.

Where was I? I'm talking to myself. Old men generally do. Certainly, I recall old men doing it and dare say Papa would have done so, if Mama would have let him. Unluckily, he never got the chance to try her patience, so how she might have reacted to his chattering is mere guesswork; informed guesswork, but nonetheless not what happened. But as I'm not, in fact, talking to myself but to you, my friend, I'll try to make sense, for both our sakes.

Maria Zachariades was not among the favourites for the honour of giving birth to the last child. No television cameras or press reporters sought her out. Before the Barren, some four hundred thousand children were born every day and though the tide of new souls was ebbing, hour by hour, ten thousand were due after me. I was only predicted to be among the last-born. Not *the* last.

No woman had conceived for nine months. American evangelists called it divine retribution and waited to be saved. In the east, the mullahs blamed the great Shaitan of the West. India and Pakistan blamed each other. Moscow blamed everyone. China, which had long fought its citizens' natural fecundity, blamed no one and stayed silent. Science was baffled. Humans were the only species affected; and now the last of the last generation were arriving and our birth was a global event.

Buddhist monks scoured Tibet and Northern China for the last Dalai Lama, priests sought a saviour in Israel and Palestine. In the Amazon the media and the authorities battled, desperate to discover an isolated tribe where the cycle of birth continued and equally desperate to ensure any such tribe remained uncontaminated. In Kashmir, a child was torn from her mother's breast and slaughtered by a mob: She was a witch, they said. She blocked our women's bellies with clay.

That was the world awaiting me.

But to continue with introductions. How am I? Thank you for asking. I'm well as can be expected: white-haired and stiff in the joints, but physically and mentally intact. I hope you are well, but fear I can't comment on your situation, or perhaps do justice to my own. How am I? is a question that can be taken several ways, but I'll begin in the here and now, flat on my back and rubbing a bruised shoulder while gazing into the slow, dark immensity of space.

Wendy, what are those?

My helpmate has followed me up the ladder and is staring at me from the entry to the roof space. He's more agile than his bulk suggests.

Unidentified: What do you see, Kit?

Acquiring voice profile.

Kit: Come here and I'll show you.

Wendy's voice comes from a speaker in his torso. His face is a hemisphere of black acrylic. It's reflecting the light of my torch. That noise is Wendy clambering over the wooden floor to join me. This recorder doesn't have video so I'll try and be descriptive for your benefit. I'm pointing at the crack of night sky. Wendy's looking.

Unidentified: Stars. It is night.

Kit: I mean those stars, those particular stars.

I've moved to let Wendy see. The robot is staring at the sky. An image of the sky has appeared on the acrylic hemisphere.

Voice profile acquired. Identification: Wen-Di Helpmate series 4. Tagged as Wendy.

Wendy: Please indicate.

Kit: I'm tapping the cluster of stars on the screen. It's far brighter than my naked eyes can see.

Wendy: They are the Pleiades, also known as the Seven Sisters.

Kit: I've never noticed before, but Wendy's quiet, unhurried voice reminds me of Papa.

Wendy: A star cluster within the constellation of Taurus. Seven stars are visible to the human eye but many more by aid of telescope. They are four hundred light years from Earth. In Greek myth they are the daughters of Atlas and Pleione.

Kit: Wendy does not see knowledge as an ever-expanding cloud but as discrete chunks to be mined a piece at a time. He has told me nothing I didn't know but I wanted to hear his voice, and for you to hear his voice. As for the Pleiades, I would add that the name comes from the Greek word *plein*, which means to sail. The Ancient Greeks used the Pleiades' reappearance to herald the season of fair weather when it was safe to put to sea. Likewise, their departure marks the beginning of the storm-ridden months when a safe passage was far less certain.

That is my here and now: gazing at starlight. But I should begin at my beginning.

So my mother told it, I had stuck fast in her womb. The doctors waited for me to release my hold; not understanding that it was my mother who held me. My stirring in her womb was the protest of a prisoner.

My mother knew I would be her only child and was determined I should have the best start in life. Prize money of thirty million dollars was at stake. Women across the globe gave birth in tears as their dream of riches vanished and there were hasty disagreements across the time zones as the world asked how the moment of the last birth would be decided.

My rivals preceded me, emerging into the world bewildered and unaware of the hope and sadness resting upon them. Each was the last born of a family, a community, a nation. To Angola, a girl; to Russia, a son; to… In London, Maria Zachariades held fast and the cameras of Sky3D and OK Channel appeared at her bedside to record the exclusive moment.

I know all this almost by rote. Thanks to my mother's iron will, I would have the greatest reception ever given a human being, but, as she never failed to remind me, the effort nearly killed her. To India a son, to China a son… her body exhausted, my mother lay down. She had done her best for me but now nature held sway and I blindly kicked and fought to escape her, as if rehearsing for the next thirty years. In Hawaii, a Vietnamese maid was receiving an emergency Caesarean. She had been playing the same game as my mother, delaying for wealth and fame, but her physician lifted out a silent girl, noosed by her umbilical. One minute and twenty-five seconds later, screaming and red-faced, I took my first breath.

Two billion people witnessed my birth and within an hour the entire world knew my name. In laboratories across the world biologists and geneticists glanced up at TV screens, looked one to another, and then turned back to the glass phials of reluctant ova and uncomprehending sperm.

The maternity theatres darkened. Midwives washed their hands and drove home. Books of children's names became curios overnight and Nestlé withdrew its baby milk formula to ironic applause.

At my mother's breast, I gained weight; ignorant for the moment of the fuss I caused. In time, the Chinese revealed the details of the Shenyang Incident and the world learned the terrible truth. The global collapse in human fertility was not an accident of nature or the anger of a god, but caused by man and man alone.

$$\Omega$$

The pain in my shoulder has eased and I'll go down soon. That I see the faint stars of the Pleiades tells me my eyes are still good, but seeing them while lying in the roof space of my home means I am experiencing a problem that has beset humanity ever since we crawled for shelter within a cave or hollow tree.

My roof leaks.

Transcript 002

Kit: Good morning, my friend. I've slept the night. Not easily, as my shoulder is still sore. I was thinking of telling you how I would take care to separate the real from the not real: the actual from conjecture and imagination and only give one and not the other. For example, that I should speak of Papa's early death, as distinct from what his life might have been and how my parents' relationship might have changed had he reached old age. But that's a curious act of abnegation; for any man, particularly an old man, is one third what he did, one third what he denied himself and one third failure. To tell you only what happened is to give you only one third of me and to become a pedantic re-teller of facts, when by nature an old man recalls his life in parables, half-truths and justifications.

I'll try to separate truths from memory, but forgive me if I lapse.

In truth I'm afraid of thunderstorms. In truth I can browse the autonet for vidcoms of me in Mama's arms, the pair of us strobe-lit by flashguns. I conjecture that my fear of thunderstorms is the awakening of a memory from when I was briefly the centre of the world's gaze. We all try to make sense of our lives.

Papa was the most innocent man I ever knew. Maria Zachariades was two months pregnant when they first met. And before I was born, listener, he married her. Such hatred he received, many assumed he married the mother of the last-born man solely for the prize of thirty million dollars. But remember, I was not meant to *be* the last-born and he could not have known how my mother would seize the moment. He married my mother because he loved her and she eternally abused his love, though he would hate me for saying so. Before the age of two or three when I can date my first memory, I've only stories that in the retelling have gained the solidity of memory. Thirty million dollars bought property and protection, and in time enough was left to buy a home on this island where now I live alone. Not for me the nursing homes where the aged tend the decrepit and automated systems wash and feed the patient, remove human waste, and, in time, cremate the human remains. My mother's efforts spared me that.

Ω

Kit: There's an Aleppo pine on the track behind my house. The track follows a ravine, bone dry in summer. A torrent in winter and spring. Two winters ago, it flooded and washed out the coast road. There haven't been any working vehicles on the island for ten years. East of my home, you come to Servos, an abandoned village below the mountains. South, beyond the broken bridge, is Marathias. Once it was the island's main town and port, but it too is abandoned. Six kilometres to the north, a spur leads off the coast road to the old lighthouse at Karithea.

Eight thousand once lived on this island, but now there's only me. There's a reliable well at Servos and the olive grove is healthy. At Karithea there's nothing, and Marathias I avoid. I grow what I can. Trapping rabbits. Sea fishing. There are lemon trees. An olive grove. I have a storehouse of dried and canned goods. I do not go hungry.

This particular Aleppo isn't tall, or perhaps I should say, not yet tall. In its early years the Aleppo grows conically: that is with a broad base growing to a point and the lowest branches only a short distance above the roots. Later, as the tree rises, the lower branches die back and fall and in maturity it will possess a long trunk crowned with an unruly nest of branches and needles.

Each year's growth of needles appears healthy and I expect great things from it. It has been growing fifteen years and I quite clearly recall when it was not there, for I equally remember the time I first saw the brush of needles held aloft on a flimsy stem. That part of the tree: the part at my feet, is the oldest. The bark there is wrinkled and calloused: ageing quite differently from a man who grows old from the head down.

I'll never see this tree grow tall. No one will.

Aleppo is only good for firewood. The timber rots easily and the pine resin means it's hard to work. I require oak; and oak should be worked green. When it's green the edge of a steel tool cuts easily, the soft shavings curling away like butter. Butter! I haven't tasted that in years. A woman at Servos used to make it from her goats. She has been dead ten years. The descendants of her goats run wild, but I've failed to bring any here. They're too good at escaping. So, no butter. Where was I? Oak. Yes. As the oak dries it naturally contracts and hardens, improving the integrity of any joints. Inevitably it will often develop splits that sometimes resemble shakes; however, unlike shakes, the splits are usually shallow and do not weaken the timber. The oak frame of my house rests on concrete pads and is flexible enough to survive anything except severe earthquake.

I have a small converter powered by seawater. I no longer trust it to run overnight and of course my solar panels require sunlight. Turning the converter on, I've instant, if limited, electrical power without draining my fuel cells. Wendy is standing on the porch. His back is covered with solar cells and if I've no orders for him, he'll remain there for hours, turning occasionally to follow the sun.

Unidentified: Jesus H Khristos!

Acquiring voice profile.

Kit: Meet the third member of my household, an African grey parrot. His name is Billybones, though I can't remember why I called him that.

Unidentified: Nee-naw, nee-naw, skkkrrrrrr!

Kit: I doubt that translates in any language you speak, my friend. Parrots are mimics, copying sounds they hear, including the human voice and the random noises of the street. I haven't heard an emergency siren in twenty years. Nor has he, but it has stuck in his vocabulary more than mine. He's happy with pine nuts and a number of cones keep him busy for hours. Parrots are one of the few animals with a lifespan similar to that of a human. In the early years of the Barren dogs and cats were the pets of choice, particularly dogs, whose dependence on a human mirrors that of a child.

I buried my last dog fifteen years ago. There are wolves on mainland Greece but they haven't reached the islands.

You shut up.

Voice profile acquired. Identification: Psittacus erithacus. Tagged as Billybones.

Billybones: Shut up!

Kit: No, you shut up.

I've given Billybones a pine cone and now I'm walking down to the sea. The morning is cool and damp. I want for human company, but have only music. It compensates. You can hear it too. I'll command it: Mozart's Requiem. External speakers.

Takes a moment for the machine to process. There. Hear that? That is some of the finest music ever made.

The stone pines hang their branches and weep resinous droplets from their needles. A low mist covers the sea and the waters are still. I'd photograph it for you, but I dropped my camera years back and it doesn't work anymore.

Two mornings ago, I found a fallen branch a few metres from the house. It had fallen from an ancient chestnut that each year sweetens my autumn. The branch was dead; the wood made surprisingly light by the fungal attack eating away at its strength. I thought it had done no damage. I was wrong. I should have lopped that branch months ago. I've paid for it now.

Habit has worn a smooth path from my door to the jetty. The wooden planks of the jetty are cool and damp. My boat lies alongside. Its hull is white and the red sails are stowed against the mast and spars.

I need to swim. I start every day in the manner of my first: naked and surprised by the cold. I'd better switch you off.

Transcript 003

Kit: As I said, I didn't sleep well last night but it was not entirely my shoulder keeping me awake. The roof needs fixing, of course, but it wasn't that either, though I'm not looking forward to it. No, it was a memory resurrected by stargazing. But if I'm to tell this in any order then it will have to wait.

I never knew my natural father and despite my questions, some at age ten, others, more insistent, at age twenty-five and again not long before Mama's death, I know nothing of him now. One half of the bloodline that led to me is blank and as I am the last of the bloodline, the absolute last to be born, that amuses me.

But if heredity is blood alone we should still be living in the trees. Ideas and culture are the true heritage of man and on that score my adopted father gave me all I needed.

He loved Bach, Beethoven and Mahler. Mama refused to have Wagner in the house. I didn't end up sharing his taste. Choral music, Mozart, and especially Jean Sibelius became my passions. But Papa taught me to listen and to seek out, not to settle for what life wanted to give me. At first, when everyone assumed the Barren wouldn't last, I gave little thought for what was filling my head. But later, as I grew into my teens and no child had been born after me, I wanted to know only the best of everything, citing Kant and Nietzsche without understanding either. I suppose that was better than some. A good many of my generation went off the rails completely. We were, in our way, the last hurrah of humanity. We were also humanity's last hope: it was for us to find a way; or at least, the future came down to us. Every parent wishes for a grandchild and collectively we failed. Not everyone can deal with that.

But you know all this and I have no special perspective. This is meant to be my story, or what I can remember of it.

Halfway through my first year at school there was a tragedy. It was the day after the Christmas holiday: only five years into the Barren, we still celebrated Christmas. It was morning and outside the school hall two women and a man were gathering in the first years. Calm hands reached out and shepherded us away from the assembly hall doors. I knew the teachers' faces but they were unfamiliar: they taught the older years. Some days Miss Bramble was unwell and another teacher had to take her class. I thought this was one of those days.

The calm hands brushed us into a smaller room. All my classmates were there. Some of them were crying or were white-faced. I was the youngest in my class and sometimes it told. I knew there was a reason we were there; I knew something had happened and no one had told me because I was the youngest.

Jenny was my friend. Jenny had a face that wouldn't smile. I grabbed her arm, wanting to know what was happening. She glared at me and pushed my arm away. She said Miss Bramble had gone to Heaven. I said she couldn't have because she wasn't old enough. Jenny said she'd heard it from her mother, so it must be true, and Miss Bramble killed herself because there won't be any more children to teach.

Jenny said it was my fault, so I sat in the corner and cried. Miss Bramble was pretty. People like her didn't die. She was the very first person who died on me. Someone said she cut her wrists in the bath. I don't know what to believe.

Everyone said how awful it was. She'd known she would lose her job because there would be no more first years to teach. Through my tears I knew I was to blame. I was the last-born: God hated me so much he couldn't bear to make any more. Jenny was right. It was my fault.

Weeks later, we learned her boyfriend had left her. She hadn't meant to kill herself, only to make him come back. It was nothing to do with me, or the Barren.

Ω

Kit: I've put on my overalls and a pair of gloves and I'm looking for a piece of oak to repair the damaged timber in the roof. This piece will do. Putting it on my sawhorse to cut it to section. Shoulder's still sore. My personal repairs will have to wait. I'm marking the wood ready to cut it.

I'm low on firewood for the winter. The heat exchanger isn't enough for the cold months. Dry grass or resin from the pine trees, flint and steel, and a supply of firewood; that I will trust.

I'm cutting. The saw blade trails a fine dust on the floor. I'm using fish oil to ease the blade through the wood. Hear that? Not my sawing – the birdsong. There's a rock thrush somewhere in the pines. The sun's burnt the sea mist away and it's warmer.

No talking. Just work for a while.

…

I've sawn the timber to the width of the piece I'm taking out. It's over-length, but I'll cut that once I'm on the roof. Despite what I said about green oak this piece is bone dry and I've spent the last ten minutes sharpening the saw. It would have been absurd to fell an oak or even lop a branch for so small a repair, even had I been fit enough to do so. Done enough for now. Brush myself down, wipe the sweat off my face. Must be careful not to make my shoulder any worse. I'd better take a rest for a bit.

Wendy?

He's lifting his head and turning to me.

Wendy: Responding.

Kit: I need you to gather firewood from the forest. Take the small cart. You know what to do, yes?

Wendy: Wendy knows criteria for firewood.

Kit: Good.

There are so many things to do and too few hours each day. Remaining among the living occupies more and more of my time and my thoughts.

Transcript 004

Kit: It's been hard work, but I have a ladder up the side of the roof, which is pitched almost from ground level to eight metres. Ropes from the head of the ladder are tied to nearby trees to stop it sliding. The ladder is aluminium. When exposed to oxygen the surface of aluminium oxidises in a layer one atom thick, protecting the metal from decay. Abrasion, inevitably, damages the oxide layer and it has to keep reforming, but as I'm the chief cause of any wear, and my ladder will certainly survive me, I think it may then last forever. I've taken the safety line off the boat. Once on the roof I'll tie myself to the ladder.

I don't fear heights, but I have respect for them. I'm not looking forward to this, but I've no choice. The ladder is flexing under me. My tools are in a bag slung across my back, but the strap keeps slipping and the bag is getting in my way. Take it slowly. Wish I hadn't sent Wendy to get firewood. Feeling alone. Concentrate on climbing, one rung to the next. Don't look down, or up. Nearly there. Can see the damage now. The mirror of what I saw last night. Sun glaring off the silvered cedar shingles and a dark hole surrounded by smashed timber. Push the tool bag out the way. Got the shackle. Undoing the thread and hooking it round the ladder rung. Tightening. At least I cannot fall.

I need to save as much as I can and reuse it. Nails, Wooden shingles. Nails especially. Jemmy the shingles off the broken timber beneath. I can only reach so far. Had to guess where I needed the ladder and I should have rested it further over. Too awkward doing this from below, from inside the roof. Reach as far as I can. A shingle comes up and slides down the roof before I can catch it. I can nearly see the edge of the beam supporting the broken stringer. Only a little more. I'm pressed so close to the ladder the rungs pinch into my chest. Rest a moment.

An onshore breeze bends the tops of the pine trees. The sea breaks into a thousand points of borrowed light tumbling toward me and extinguishing on the shore. The breeze strips the sweat from my back and the sun burns through my shirt. Have to go on.

I'm leaning over, jemmy in hand, trying to reach the last of the shingles. The broken stringer is clear from one rafter to the next. Have to cut it out and replace with new wood. Hanging the jemmy on the ladder a moment. Need the saw now. My feet hurt from standing on the narrow rung. I want a rest, but only this small part to do. Once I do this I can get down. Tool bag is filled with the shingles I pulled off. They're jamming together. Hard to get the saw out. Damn it, come out! This is – Shit! Oh fuck no!

…

I'm still here. Mouth full of blood, but still here.

Saw caught on the bag and it jerked round me. The ladder shifted. Only by a half metre, but enough to throw my feet off the rung and leave me dangling by the safety strap. I've got my feet back on the ladder now. Just hoping the ropes hold and the ladder stays where it is.

Cut my arm on the saw. Stings like hell.

Need to stop a moment. Get my nerve back. Need to get down. Can't talk and do this.

$$\Omega$$

Kit: Wendy! Wendy. Here.

Wendy: You are hurt?

Kit: I'm hurt. Help me inside. Leave the cart here.

Wendy: Kit leans too heavily.

Kit: Sorry.

Wendy: Thank you. My servos cannot maintain balance.

Kit: I understand. When we're inside, bring me the first aid stuff.

Wendy: Will respond.

Kit: Here's the door. I can stand, but I'm unsteady. Need a hand on Wendy's shoulder. Chair. Sitting down. Oh God this is messy. Waiting for Wendy. Need to patch myself up. Enough talking.

Ω

Kit: The ladder leans drunkenly across the roof. The small hole of last night is now a long expanse of darkness where I stripped off the shingles to get at the timber beneath. I'm gathering my things slowly. The pain in my shoulder is, for the moment, forgotten. The cut where I caught my arm on the saw is shallow but it feels as though the flesh is on fire. Also I wrenched my wrist, cut my lip and bruised my shin. I can't do any more. I'm going inside. I've a pocket full of nails. Empty them out. Can straighten them later. Better see what I look like in the mirror.

Got some rubbing alcohol. Disinfect the cut across my arm. Hurts horribly. No choice. Probably an unnecessary precaution, but I can't take the risk. I'll be stiff and sore later. Have to do as much as I can now. Make coffee. Then I'll straighten out those nails before my hands give up.

Billybones is chattering to me as I cover his cage for the night. I'm getting too old for this life but so are we all.

Transcript 005

Kit: I've decided that I'm not going to worry about the significance of the memories I share. That I remember them vividly seems enough. Daniel was my friend. It was one of those childhood friendships as intense and permanent as snow. I was seven years old. Daniel and I would part company after a year and not see each other again until twenty years later when chance made us work colleagues. As adults we had nothing in common, which was probably my fault as there were few with whom I ever felt anything in common. I don't know why he was my friend. Do we ever understand why some people attract us and others don't, or what quality others see in us? As children we were inseparable, until the day he said he'd something to show me.

He said it in such a way as to make whatever it was seem irresistible and when Mama arrived after school to take me home I hid behind a hedge and then crept away with Daniel.

I followed a metre behind him. It was odd walking streets I didn't know, passing shops and places I didn't recognise. It was transgressive; as though I were stepping into the unknown. I kept asking what he was going to show me, but he only said how amazing it was. I was impatient, and perhaps guilty at deceiving Mama.

And it was amazing, though the effect it had on me was not what Daniel had expected or hoped for.

He turned off the road and marched up to a door, proudly saying it was his house. He had the key to the door in his pocket. This was astonishing in itself. His mother worked so wasn't there to greet him, but the house wasn't empty. A booming sound came from upstairs. His older brother never went out, but just sat in his room all the time.

We dropped our coats and bags in the hallway and Daniel led me upstairs to a door. He said the thing was inside but we had to be quiet. Given the noise coming from his brother's room, quietness seemed unnecessary. Daniel said if we were noisy she would wake up. I had no idea what he meant. He let me in.

The room was smaller than the rooms in my home. The walls were pale pink like the skin under your fingernails. There was a window and sunlight through net curtains and a cot placed just out of the sun's reach. Daniel repeated I had to be quiet, said otherwise she would start crying. Then I saw it.

I didn't know how big babies were supposed to be. I'd never seen one except in pictures and it's hard to tell. In the flesh Daniel's sister seemed huge, though all I could see was a round pink face and a blanket covering her.

Daniel said its name was Emily, then he spoke to it, asking *Em, how's Em today?* in a childish voice.

The pink head turned and its eyes opened. They were blue and bright as glass. Daniel asked me to say something to it, but I didn't want to. I said it looked weird.

The blue eyes locked on mine and the lips closed tightly.

Daniel said I wasn't to say anything unkind or I'd upset her.

The eyes moved again, sliding in their silicone sockets to look at Daniel. The mouth smiled.

Daniel said the doll had recognised him and his voice made the thing thrash its legs and squeal.

Then he said it had cost a lot of money and his mother wouldn't say how much. He said everything worked and tugged the blanket down to show me. It had a white one-piece with pink and yellow daisies and buttons that looked like ladybirds. Something smelled, like spilt orange juice. Daniel said it needed changing and asked if I wanted to watch. I did not.

Daniel shrugged and started unbuttoning the suit, saying his mother would shout at him if he ignored the doll. The skin was as lifelike as the face. I shrank back, revolted but fascinated as well. I had never seen anyone younger than me and this doll was like someone much younger.

I had seen enough and backed away. Daniel said I was weird for not wanting to look at it. I said something about hating it and the doll thrashed its arms. Then came a strange snuffling sound, like a dog eating, and a scream.

Daniel swore and blamed me for the doll crying. The noise was the most horrible thing I had ever heard and I covered my ears. Daniel slipped the suit down to the doll's waist and rolled it over. He pressed something in the middle of its back and screaming stopped. I let go my ears.

He said he wasn't supposed to do that, but act like it was really his baby sister. There was something perfunctory in the way Daniel stripped off the nappy and changed it.

I asked if it would grow any bigger. Daniel said it wasn't supposed to grow up. I said I wanted to go home.

Mama had phoned three times but I sat watching Daniel change the nappy on the doll. He was right. They'd made it with everything. It was as perfect as you could get for eight thousand Euros. I wanted to pick it up by its ankles and smash it against the wall.

Daniel said I was jealous. I didn't know what he meant. He said I had been the youngest, but wasn't the youngest any more, so I kicked him in the back of the legs. He howled and dropped the doll in the cot. It screamed.

Our noise and the screaming doll brought a sudden change. The thumping music stopped and Daniel's brother opened the door on us. He had long, straggly hair and hadn't shaved. He swore at Daniel and said his mother would be after him. Then he looked at me and swore again, asking who I was.

I said I was last. I was *the* last, not that horrible doll.

Afterwards, I sat on the wall outside Daniel's house and waited for Mama. I didn't have to wait long. She pulled up and opened the car door without a word. I crept in. She didn't say anything or even look at me. Mostly you could never stop

Mama talking but when she was her angriest or most hurt she never said a word.

It's night now. Aching everywhere but I'm not sleepy. There's so much to do and so little time. Keep thinking what if I'd fallen? Fallen but not died, for death is too easy. What would I have done? I'm longing for the coming winter to be over, but when it ends I must work and work.

Sorry. You don't need to hear that. I'm always complaining. Many would be thankful for the life I've had. I knew what was in prospect for the many; I'd helped design some of it. And I'm not alone, I have Wendy and Billybones: life could be much worse. And I have you, mysterious stranger, hearing my voice countless years in the future.

I'm miserable tonight: maudlin, even. Dragging up painful memories. I'm turning you off. I need to sit a while, free of the sound of my own voice. Tired of explaining myself, tired of making sense out of life. There's no sense. No meaning. There never was. Goodnight.

Transcript 006

Kit: The Aegean isn't tideless.

I'm drifting southward at one-half knot, measuring my progress against the abandoned lighthouse at Karithea. The wind is driving me toward the shore and twice I've drawn in my fishing lines, set my sails and beaten away to sea.

I'm drifting in a surface current. It's fed by rivers which in turn are fed by the rain and meltwaters of the Southern Alps. It carries me like the marker in a falling barometer. Yet it's deceptive, for there's a current of heavier, saltier water flowing northward as the sea creeps toward high tide.

I've abandoned the roof for the day. Too many aches and pains to go up the ladder again. Fishing relaxes me and, except when I must work the sails, it's not arduous.

As a small child I recall visiting the River Thames in London and thinking it so big it must be the sea. Twice daily it would flood upriver beneath the bridges, fill its course, and twice daily it would empty, exposing shimmering mud. Here, on the Aegean where I've made my home, the tidal range is far less, only a few tenths of a metre.

According to evolutionary theory the inter-tidal zone was a crucial staging post during the emergence of land animals. Once, among the sea's debris, our ancestors made a home.

I'm drifting southward on the surface current and my hooks are trailing northward in the salt. I've caught three sea bass using shellfish for bait.

I've always loved the sea. No. That isn't quite true. I've always feared it, a little. And we're fascinated by that which excites a little awe in us. I caught the fascination from Papa. I would take the jib sheet and scurry across the bows as the boat heeled on a new tack. He held the tiller and the mainsheet and would chide me for lacking attention. I had always an eye for the sea and the view of the coast; its horizontals of water and beach and the row of guesthouses and hotels beyond.

He would warn me when he was about to tack and then the stern slewed in the water and the boom swung above Papa's head. I would loosen the jib sheet and with the sail cracking and whipping above my head, I'd clamber across to the other side of the boat and jam the rope in the cleat. Papa would tell me I was too slow. I was always too slow.

The boat was *Sea Otter*. Papa would lower it down a slipway and then we'd sail up and down the shoreline. He was happy where he was, doing what he did. He had Mama and he had me. He didn't want for anything more. But Easter was different, as though Papa found more daring. We always holidayed in Dorset. My father claimed his family came from there, way back when. I never knew if this was true or just an excuse for staying at Weymouth where we'd sail somewhere new every day, though hardly ever venturing beyond the bay. He would tell me stories of the tide race off Portland Bill and for once I would pay attention to the sea and where we were going, anxious not to get too near The Bill. I feared it like a ferocious dog, ready to leap out and upset us. I live by the sea, yet I've never wholly lost that fear. The dog is still out there, waiting, and even on a day like this my eye is on the windward horizon, watching for any change that might herald bad weather.

We also went to far more exotic places. We had the money and Papa said we should see the world while we still could. Most places were still safe to travel but he knew it wouldn't stay like that for long. He was right. Yet despite seeing much of the world, it's the weeks in Weymouth I best remember.

The last time we sailed together I was sixteen. The bow of the *Sea Otter* was too small for me and I had become a moody and uncooperative sailor and didn't much help my father when we brought the boat out of the water onto the slip. What should have been easy for two fell on my father and suddenly he bent double over the bow, as though he'd been struck. The weight of the boat fell on me and brought me out of my sullenness. I stopped the trailer rolling into the sea. Papa leant against the harbour wall. I had never seen him so pale.

He said I had to call Mama. I asked if it was his back. He repeated I had to call Mama. So I did and I told her Papa was ill. I didn't know what he was ill with; just that she had to come get us.

I told Papa I'd done as he asked and I asked him what was hurting. He didn't know. Except he'd never felt so bad before.

The local doctor gave him painkillers, but there was no more sailing with Papa, not ever.

I must try not to get ahead of myself. I'll tell all this another day. One memory of sailing is the wind chafing my arms and face to scarlet and Mama worrying at my skin with liniment. I hadn't inherited her dark complexion. I burned easily, still do. I think I've said enough for now.

$$\Omega$$

Kit: I've landed ten sea bass and the lighthouse at Karithea is falling astern. It won't be many weeks before the Pleiades sink below the horizon for another season. I'll gut the fish and cook one for supper. The rest I'll smoke with cedar wood.

Transcript 007

Kit: The path is more memory than fact. In this season it runs beside a torrent of dry stones. Water slides between them and gathers in dark pools. The oak trees cluster in the foot of the valley where there's damp and shade. In turn, they're shading my back. The stones of the path are sharp through the soles of my boots.

I'm going to Servos, the old village in the hills. I have an olive grove there. It was once home to Theodore Zenakthis, a dentist by trade. Born in Servos, he returned there when the city grew untenable. He was twenty years older than I was. Years ago, I made this journey in agony from an abscess growing beneath a tooth. It was spring and the river was in spate. It was a hard journey. Theodore was furious when he examined me. The tooth had been painful for three weeks before I called on him. He pulled the tooth and drained the abscess. I caught a fever and had to stay a week with him to recover. The abscess was poisoning my blood. If I had waited another week before seeking him I wouldn't have survived.

It was soon after that, he asked me to bury him when the time came, and I couldn't refuse. Yet when I called on him at the end of that summer to help harvest the olives, he'd gone. His cottage was as he'd left it, but his black-faced sheep were scarce surviving on the scant grass in their pasture. I sensed he hadn't been about for some days, or weeks even. I walked all the paths I knew he kept, but found no sign. His body must lie somewhere up in the hills. No one wants to lie down at the end like a beast. All I could do for him was follow one wish. I broke down the wattle fence and released his sheep. He said they'd fend for themselves and I could take what I needed for meat.

And so nature reclaimed her own, one way or another. Save for a yearling that gave me mutton for a month.

Thinking of the Pleiades the other night. I first saw the stars the night before we arrived in Kastoria. I was nine years old. My mother's aunt had died and we were there for her funeral.

The plane was late landing at Makedonia Airport. I remember the vivid orange of the sunset and the glow on the white buildings. The man in the car hire centre protested through a cigarette. His wife was expecting him home. He should have closed up, he said in bad English.

Mama pushed her elbows onto the counter and spat Greek at him. Papa looked ashamed.

Afterwards in the car lot she said my father didn't know how to deal with people. Papa said nothing, but took the car keys. I sat in the rear seat and stared at the back of my parents' heads. The roads were narrow and ill-repaired; they took us through a dry landscape. Goats wandered free at the roadside. The sky grew dark. I stretched out on the back seat.

I was seven when Papa told me that I had another father, somewhere, but Mama would never answer my questions and my natural father would remain a mystery.

The man I called Papa had long realised that patience was his only choice if he was to hold onto my mother, and he loved her enough to be so. He was always terrified that one day she wouldn't be there, that she would find another more her equal. He strived to make that as difficult as possible by being perfect. It never occurred to him that one day he might leave her. But I digress. That night on the road to Kastoria my father's cancer was many years away.

West of Fanós the road breaks its back in hairpins before crossing a dry pass and then descending to Vérga and Lake Kastoria. The motion of the car on those tight bends woke me and I leant my head against the window. High hills pressed against the road. Stones and bent trees loomed in the headlight beams.

I asked where we were. Papa said he didn't know. Mama said he knew perfectly well and we were nearly there. The car pitched into another bend and my head pressed against the window glass. My throat dried as though I had sucked on chalk. I said I felt sick. Mama ordered Papa to stop the car. Papa protested because there was nowhere to stop. He didn't know the road, he didn't know the country. Mama insisted, saying otherwise they'd have to pay for someone to clean the car.

The car was black, a ridiculous shade for the hot weather, but Mama insisted on the colour because of the funeral. Perhaps it was the heat in the car earlier in the day that left me feeling sick. Outside, it was surprisingly cold. I had no shoes on and the gravel at the roadside hurt my feet. Opening the doors worked the car's interior light and Mama's shadow jerked in it like a puppet, her voice tripping between Greek and London English as she forced my head down to be sure nothing splashed on my feet.

Lavender growing in the shade of the wall had crushed beneath the car tyres and the scent filled the air. I tried to retch, but it's hard to be unwell when lavender fills your lungs.

Then Papa turned off the headlights and closed the car door, leaving us in darkness.

Mama asked what he was doing. Papa's voice replied gently, saying he had an idea. There was something I had never seen before.

Mama must have understood him because I felt her fingers reach from my shoulder into my dark hair. The cold got into my feet and I scrunched them up, as if to separate myself from the reality of the cold road. Then I saw the stars.

My parents and I lived in a quiet London suburb where the streets glowed all night long and the sky was orange even through my curtain-drawn sleep; but on that road in Greece the stars blazed down. I hope I said nothing, but I doubt it. I almost certainly whispered something. In North London Papa had shown me three *stars* not our sun: Venus, and Jupiter and Saturn, and perhaps Mars.

In Greece, these other stars shone bright and steady above the hills.

Papa said it was cold because we were high in the hills and the land lost its heat quickly after dark. My father was the kind of man who had to speak something out loud to understand it.

The stars I saw that night were impossible to consider individually. At the highest arc there were so many they merged into a bridge that curved from one dry hillside to the other. Papa called it the Milky Way. I had never heard of it before. Now it's my nightly friend.

Mama's hand rocked my head as if to deny Papa's truth and then her mouth brushed my face as she said there was a new star in Heaven, burning for my aunt, Mama's beloved sister, who had left us and gone to be with God. Mama said she was up there looking down at us.

Behind her voice I could hear my father's footstep, I don't know in which direction. I cannot remember more of that night. I can barely remember the funeral, except for the black clothes and the heat in the day.

Strange the things we remember. Want to be quiet for a while.

Ω

Kit: This is Servos. That noise is the cicadas. I'm sitting by the well. The pump doesn't work, but I've a bucket on a rope. Water's cool and sweet. The last person who lived here is buried by the ruined church. I knew her, though she was already aged when I arrived on the island. She feared that I would evict her and I had to persuade her my patch of land didn't extend so far. People thought I had bought the whole island, not just a pocket of land from the mayor. Now, I'm walking to the church, bucket in hand. The woman died twelve years ago. I want to find the grave where Theodore and I laid her and pour some of the water on the ground. The olive grove was her husband's. It's now mine.

There are other graves by the church, each marked by a mound of earth. I don't know their owners. The village was already dying when the Barren came. The old stayed, the young fled to the cities. Three years ago an earthquake brought down the church tower and every season another crack runs up the old walls. Every year a roof beam fails and the red tiles cascade down into the narrow streets. I'm glad Theodore lies up in the hills. Better nature has him than this ruin.

Here it is. A libation for you, old woman. I cannot recall your name. Forgive me.

The olive trees mind themselves much of the year. They survive drought well. I prune the old wood best I can. I don't prune so many of the trees as I once did. It's hard work and my limbs aren't what they were. The fruit grows on the green wood. I'm not here to prune or harvest. I wanted to see when they'll be ready. Two months, I think. The harvest will be good this year. It varies, without any reason I know, but this year will be good. Going inside to check the olive press. Giving it a turn. It's stiff. It's taking all my weight to get it going. There! Hear that? Gearing still works. Winding it up. Concrete block is coming off the press. Won't take it any further. It's working, that's all that matters. Winding it back down so the weight isn't on the gears.

Wendy will bring up the empty canisters for the oil. Climbing up into the roof space. Everything looks sound. I don't care if the rest of Servos falls down, so long as this building stands. Without a press, I have no oil. No beams of sunlight disturb the darkness. The roof is sound.

I've done everything I came for.

Transcript 008

Kit: The weather's holding. I've not been up on the roof since the accident. I should finish the repair, yet each time I look at the ladder I shudder and walk on. It's not the fall I fear; I lack trust in my own limbs. Also, my bruises remain. I rediscovered this too, the cost of an ill-night's sleep. If I'm weary in body,

I'm weary in spirit also. Wendy has many skills but he doesn't know when a man needs encouragement and company.

In any event, fate isn't yet done with me. This morning I discovered a still worse disaster. Or rather, Wendy brought it to my attention. My supply of salt is ruined.

Salt is my sole means of preserving meat and fish and making bread palatable. I've repaired my refrigeration unit so often I think next time I won't be able to fix it. Salt is dependable. But there's nowhere sheltered enough for a saltpan on this island so I must barter for it.

I'm walking through the storehouse with Wendy. Salt crystals glitter on the concrete floor. Water got in during the same storm that damaged my roof. Nothing else is damaged.

Wendy: You have not lost all the salt.

Kit: Enough is lost. What's left won't get me through winter.

Wendy: Then you should acquire it. You acquire salt from Andreas Alexandris. He has more salt than he needs.

Kit: I know where to get salt.

Andreas lives on an island two days away. I can't ignore the lost salt, but Andreas's company unsettles me.

I need not go to him, yet. I shall leave in a day or two.

Wendy: Why delay? It is unlike you.

Kit: Don't claim to know what I'm like.

Wendy: Salt harmful to Wendy's components.

Kit: Salt, especially damp salt is corrosive. You'd better go. I'll clean this up.

Wendy: Do you have instructions for me?

Kit: No instructions. Correction. Firewood, as yesterday.

The robot's going, leaving me alone with the mess. It's childish but I'll not have him idle while I'm working. I've come out of the storehouse to see what else needs repairing. A length of gutter has fallen down. How can something so small have such heavy consequences?

$$\Omega$$

Kit: I've brought buckets of seawater up to wash out the storeroom floor. Swept it clear. Everything is wet, but it'll dry out quickly. I leave the door open. The salt's stripped the skin from my hands. Skin's cracked. The smell is vile and I feel wretched. I've stopped working and just sit on my knees. Feeling dreadful. Excuse me.

...

Sorry. You didn't need that. Been ill. Waiting for my head to clear. Feeling my age. The youngest man in the world is feeling his age. What does that say about me? Got the bucket and I'm walking down to the shore to fill it. Life is hard and I'm not as able as I was. The prospect of two days' sail to Andreas is worrying me. Life is hard; things must be done and there's only one escape and I'm not yet ready for that. Daniel was right. For those who wanted it there were pills, and suicide machines and God knows what else, and no shame in using them. People wanted control of their lives to the very end. You bought suicide pills on prescription. A doctor had to agree to it. Later, I forget which year it was, everyone got them, like centenarians getting a letter from the King. The unwritten rule was, don't leave an inconvenient corpse. Sea cruises were popular. I'm getting ahead of myself. That was the second time I knew Daniel. After the doll. Years later when we worked at the same company. Trying to tell this in some sort of order, but memory doesn't work like that.

I hope to drop dead one day, suddenly and without pain. Wendy will bury me, release the parrot and close up the house. Without my instruction, he'll have no more purpose. He'll shut down: his end following mine. That's my hope. My fear is the same we all had: a painful and incapacitating end. If that happens, Wendy knows where I keep those pills. But before then, these things I need to know: how to repair a roof, make salt from water, and trim the wick of a lamp. We didn't teach children those skills. I can still name fifty capital cities, the world's oceans, key dates of history: dead facts, dead knowledge. They didn't know what else to teach us. Now I can tie a bowline in the dark and gut a fish without thinking about it. That I have use for.

Fill the bucket. Returning to the storeroom to clean up after myself. I'm rambling but sometimes talk takes my mind off things. Our teachers knew we would need to know other things. In my eleventh year I remember a teacher said Europe would be over-run by Africans. He drew charts showing how far young blacks outnumbered young whites. We had a rapidly ageing population, sub-Saharan Africa a relatively youthful population. Someone asked if we could stop them with guns. Someone suggested we had nuclear missiles. The teacher, I think his name was Roberts, said that if the Africans didn't come we would beg them and pay them to come. Who else but the young would care for the infirm; who would care for him?

The idea of Britain overrun by Africans was unpopular with the school governors. He left.

Mrs Drake in religious education talked a lot about God and what God was to other people. Why God had done this to us, if he ever existed, went unanswered. Mama raised me in the Greek Orthodox Church, just as she'd promised her mother she would. I don't think I ever believed. I don't think Mrs Drake really believed.

I'm still carrying all that stuff. So much dead weight. Who we were seems scarcely relevant any more. I'm an old man feeding pine nuts to a parrot while talking to a nameless being he'll never meet. Need to turn this off.

Ω

Kit: I've been silent for hours. Night's fallen. I was weak and self-pitying earlier. Forgive me. It's hard to bear one's mortality, since it's the mortality of us all, an entire race grown old. Seeing Andreas may be good for me. I'm spending too much time on my own. Though he's no different. And I've no choice for I must have salt. Is optimism so foolish? Perhaps, but without it I'd be dead by now.

The sky's clear tonight and the Pleiades have risen. Still the time for voyaging.

Transcript 009

Kit: The Barren was no barrier to desire, at least not for a man. At fifteen I fell in love, or at least fell into lust.

Hannah was a few weeks older than I and philosophical about the age difference. When I told her, perhaps boastfully, that I was the last-born, she gave me a strange, disbelieving look. There was rain in her hair. Her face was lowered, her eyes hidden behind her fair lashes, and her mouth closed and serious. We had escaped the weather among the books of a public library.

Hannah pushed me back against the tall wooden shelving and told me she and I were lucky to be alive. Then she kissed me as a million things I would never know pressed against my spine.

She was right, of course. Had the Shenyang Incident been one week, or even a day earlier, the infection might have reached my mother before I was conceived. This truth had never occurred to me before. Hannah was right: I was lucky to be alive.

When Jean Sibelius composed his fourth symphony he was ill with what he believed was throat cancer. He later said that the earliest ideas for the work came to him while on holiday in Finland with his brother-in-law, a painter who worked at his easel while the composer walked in the nearby forest. Sibelius, a staunch Finnish nationalist, drew on landscape for much of his inspiration, but in his fourth the northern forest seems darker, more baleful, than in any other work. In my imagination it's a forest in mid-winter, the trees bent by the weight of snow.

Snow is rare on my coast but inland, among the mountains, the winter rains often turn to snow.

Sibelius completed the fourth symphony and four more. The cancer was a misdiagnosis. Later, when still only in his middle age but out of sympathy with modern music, he destroyed his final great work, the eighth symphony, and for his last three decades wrote nothing. More useless knowledge.

Nothing lasts forever.

Sitting in the corner of a cafe Hannah reassured herself that she would never want children and asked me if I felt the same. I said we didn't have a choice. She was certain the Barren wouldn't last, that it was only a matter of time and money before they found a cure. I said maybe and drank my coffee.

The cafe was full of students. Noisy, feet on chairs; and iridescent hair. The Barren dominated talk for hours on end. We were the last generation and we were special. The cafe was our home.

Budgets for fertility research rivalled armament spending, and, released from the burden of child-raising, women had closed the wage gap on men.

At fifteen Hannah and I went our separate ways. I didn't see her again. Why do I remember her? Only now, speaking to you, do I recall so much. I'm not sure it's healthy, all this remembering. Nothing lasts forever and perhaps it's best that way. Time to work.

$$\Omega$$

Kit: It's two days' sailing to Andreas's island. The first day hugging the coast of my own island, and the second crossing eighty kilometres of open sea. Eighty kilometres is dawn to sunset in my boat, providing no adverse winds. If I meet a storm – and it's not impossible – it could blow me many kilometres off course. Need food and water, especially water, for minimum four days.

I'm on the boat checking everything's working. Can't risk anything breaking at sea. The sails run freely up and down the mast. Ropes all look okay. Rudder swings easily. Should go below the boat and check the hull. Wendy went to the well at Servos and brought back fifty litres. I praised him but he ignored me. You cannot thank a robot for carrying out your order. It doesn't understand gratitude. Half of the water is aboard and I've got dried food in the lockers. That's more than enough for four days, but I may need more than that. Andreas is an old man. No guarantee he's still alive, or has spare food for me. I'm unaccountably worried, even though I've sailed to Andreas many times. Is age creeping up on me? One day I won't be physically able and there's only Wendy to care for me. Best ignore such thoughts. I have instructions for my tin man.

Wendy?
Wendy: Attending.
Kit: Good. What must you do while I am away?
Wendy: Feed Billybones and keep the house safe.

Kit: Correct. And if I have not returned after one month?

Wendy: Release Billybones. Put out food for him for one further month. Then assume Kit not coming back. Close the house and sleep.

Kit: But I will come back. I will always come back.

Ω

Kit: Back on the boat finishing everything. Starting to repeat myself. Checking what I've already done. Why reassure the robot that I'll return? Will my fate make any difference beyond triggering a program? Wendy cannot understand grief. The parrot will feel more sorrow at my passing: the sorrow of having to find its own pine cones. Grief is the need to fend for oneself. Grief is being alone.

The boat's as ready as it can be. Leaving it for tonight. Tomorrow night I'll be sleeping at Marathias. I don't usually go ashore there. The army evacuated everyone over sixty to the mainland ten years ago. I was under the age limit. A few more escaped by hiding in the hills. Marathias is falling into ruins and there's nothing worth taking. But I suppose I can say something about the place, and the people I knew there.

You'll make me talkative, my friend.

Transcript 010

Kit: It's late and I can't sleep. I'll talk for a while.

The fuss over my birth disappeared for some years. I was almost forgotten. That changed when I was eighteen. At eighteen people listen to you, or pretend to.

I was sitting in the back of a taxi paid for by Channel Nine. It was night in North London. A crowd picketed the studio. In God Our Trust, and God's Will Be Done, said the placards.

The taxi driver said they were idiots and asked if they wanted man to go extinct. I didn't have an answer for him.

In the brief moment I had before we turned down a side street I didn't think them dangerous. A man who carries a slogan rarely carries anything else.

The cab stopped beside a steel door in an otherwise featureless wall. The driver passed a sheaf of paper to the woman PA sitting alongside me. She signed a page and passed it back.

The driver glanced at her signature and left. I don't think he knew who I was.

As the PA shepherded me through the door, I heard shouts from the protesters at the entrance and asked if there'd be any trouble. She said, they'll make the news, which is all they want.

She led me along a narrow corridor lined with plain wooden doors. At some point the floor became carpeted and the plain doors were name tagged. When art works appeared on the walls, I knew we had reached the building's public face.

The PA pushed open a door for me and asked me to wait inside. Make-up would collect me when I was needed. Meanwhile, there was coffee. One wall of the room had windows onto a courtyard. I could smell hot coffee and the walls were lined with sofas. A man in a grey suit crossed the room, reached for my hand and pumped it mechanically as he greeted me. Then he introduced me to the other guests.

My fame had mostly burned out in my childhood. I was the only one not immediately recognisable. Fortunately, or not, my name is memorable and when Archbishop Heywood shook my hand he said I must have a personal perspective on Professor Baxter's work.

I warmed to him, but said that so far as I was concerned being the last-born was never much of a career and I was happy to pass it on now.

The archbishop wore a black robe and though he was over fifty his hair was also black. Like many, he refused to go grey. Professor Geraint Baxter was the only man in the room who had grey hair. He was also the tallest. The PA introduced me formally to the other guests and then left us alone.

The zoologist, Monique Lefoy, kissed me on both cheeks in the French fashion. I had seen her on television. She had beauty and brains, but I knew little about her. The philosopher David Hayton I had met once before for a radio recording. He was thin and his clothes hung off him as though he were airing them. His head was shaved and he wore a skull cap.

He had this way of holding his palms together and bowing when he greeted you. I said hello in reply and admitted I felt unqualified in all the company.

Hayton laughed and said I wasn't to worry. He said my position was unique and while a number of people could take his role in tonight's programme, there was only one last-born man.

Then I was standing next to Baxter. He shook my hand, then glanced at me thoughtfully as he poured coffee into a china cup. His eyes were sharp, and for a second I felt like a student before an unusually competent tutor. He offered me the coffee and asked if I knew why I had been invited tonight.

Professor Baxter was the country's leading geneticist. Twelve months before, a lovingly cared-for sow had been anaesthetised and its womb and ovaries removed intact. It was no ordinary swine flesh. Its chromosomes were human. Ten months later the woman who received the womb and ovaries became pregnant and we were here tonight to discuss the implications on live TV.

I had a reply to Baxter's question. I said I was the voice of the ordinary man and I would try not to make a fool of myself on camera.

If the rain had dampened the mood of the protestors outside, inside the studio under the lights, I was uncomfortably warm and the air was dry.

Archbishop Heywood, Baxter, Hayton, Lefoy and I sat in a crescent of close-spaced chairs. Black leather in a chrome frame. In front of us was a low glass-topped table and on the far side, the presenter sat in a similar chair to ours. I've never much enjoyed being in front of a crowd and tried to ignore the bank of people in the audience whose questions the presenter relayed to us.

Lefoy was speaking, her French accent more noticeable than before. She supported Baxter's work. She would have supported anything that gave us a chance to prevent our extinction. But she warned that it would be a mistake to repopulate to previous levels. The presenter tried to twist her words, but she insisted Baxter had her complete support. Her only concern was how the research might be used.

Then the presenter turned to me and asked if I supported the work, if I believed the end justified the means, however ethically questionable? I said the objections were based on squeamishness, not ethics. Any child born would be fully human, and not some hybrid because it was birthed by a pig. To lighten things, I said I should like a younger brother.

The presenter turned to Archbishop Heywood. Heywood hadn't liked my joke. He said it was unreasonable to dismiss genuine concerns as squeamishness. He said Baxter's methods might result in something that was genetically human but there was the human soul to consider. It was difficult to believe a human soul can emerge from the reproductive organs of a pig.

I was still quietly basking in the ripple of laughter from my remark about a younger brother. Baxter was leaning forward, waiting for Heywood to finish. There was a movement in the audience. Someone standing with outstretched arm. Then a gunshot. Screaming. More gunshots.

I must have scrambled to the floor. I didn't pray, I didn't scream. The glass from the shattered tabletop fell across my head and back as I curled tightly around my stomach, my hands over my head and ears. I wanted to be small, too small to see.

Then the shooting stopped. Lefoy was on the floor with her back to me. Fragments of glass in her hair. Beyond her Professor Baxter still sat in his chair, leaning forward. I got to my knees. The gunman was holding up his hands, awaiting arrest. Security men rushed down the aisles toward him. I brushed the pieces of glass from Lefoy's hair. After a few moments there was blood on my hands.

Then a hand on my shoulder startled me. It was a paramedic. He asked if I was wounded. I wasn't, except for the cuts from the glass. The man examined them and said I'd need stitches. I still have a few scars.

Hayton was helping Lefoy to her feet. There was blood on her face. Heywood was unhurt. Professor Baxter hadn't moved.

In the course of the next few minutes it was ascertained that Archbishop Heywood and the presenter were uninjured. I had minor cuts. Lefoy had broken her arm and required stitches for a cut on her chin. A paramedic examining Hayton surprised him with the news that a bullet fragment had lodged in his thigh. Two bullets hit Professor Baxter, killing him instantly. Another five shots had missed us all.

Three months later the foetus was aborted. The drugs necessary to prevent the woman rejecting the pig's womb were causing severe foetal abnormalities. All subsequent trials had the same outcome and the project was abandoned.

At his subsequent trial, the assassin pleaded guilty. Less than a year into his sentence he was murdered by a fellow inmate.

I don't suppose Baxter's death made any difference in the end. For me, I suppose it was the end of my childhood. That's enough for now. Need to sleep. Good night.

Transcript 011

Wendy: Goodbye, Kit. Wendy knows what to do.

Kit: I know you do. You'll take care now.

I dislike goodbyes. Even a goodbye to a robot is awkward and seems to last forever. I'm leaning over the stern to get the rope off the mooring pin.

Wendy: Please clarify.

Kit: No matter, talking to myself.

First sign of insanity. The second must be getting emotional over animated plastic. I've got the bow rope now. The boat is free. Pushing off with a pole. Need to get some space around me. That's enough. Can get the sail up.

Wendy: Goodbye, Kit.

Kit: He's waving at me. Can't fault what I've taught him. His voice doesn't carry across the water. I wave back before winding up the foresail. It ripples before the breeze catches and fills the sail. The boat is slipping away from the shore. Soon as I'm clear of the bay I'll get the mainsail up. I've thought of everything. Been over and over it. Hope that's not hubris speaking. Sea is an intense blue. Dazzle of the waves hurts my eyes but I'm forgetting my age for a moment. Sitting in the stern, the rudder alive in my hands. I'm back again on the *Sea Otter*, my father a shadowy form up in the bows ready with the jib sheet. I'm escaping my home. I was always escaping. I want to just be on the boat for a while. Turning you off.

Ω

Kit: At eighteen I didn't know what I wanted to do with my life. It was a common feeling. I didn't need to work. We had the money invested in trust funds and my future was cared for. Mama would have been happy for me to stay at home, but Papa insisted that everyone must have purpose, now more than ever. College beckoned and one subject stood out above all the others – Gerontics: the study of old age. Papa joked it was the only growth industry we had.

The Barren ended so many of mankind's hopes and quests but this was the challenge of our time. Mr Roberts was right: we would need every young person we could find, regardless of origin, to care for an ageing population. The only question, though one rarely addressed, was who'd care for the young when they grew old? I asked the same question: who'd care for me, the youngest of all?

I took my degree in London and within a year I knew I didn't want to be cared for by anything we could envisage. Instead, I'd take oblivion before my health failed. I wouldn't live a life I despised. I wonder what that arrogant youth would make of me now. I tire before the day is out. The hurt I got repairing, or failing to repair my roof, is taking days to heal, I forget names easily and I depend on Wendy more than I should. Now, at least, I won't depend on him for a few days.

His balance sensors can't cope with the sea: he gets disorientated. I assume the Wen-Di Corporation never thought their robots would need to go to sea.

It's only for a few days and Andreas will be company. Must get used to hearing someone speak without prompting, though Andreas's mind wanders these days and I've heard much of his life twice over. And he mine. That's what old men do: they remind each other who they are; endlessly redrawing the lines in their memory, fearful of erasure. So, where was I?

After Hannah, there was Kirstie. She was two months older than me. I always asked people their exact ages. People often said I'd never find anyone younger than me and I'd always laugh it off, and say I knew that. Knowing and wanting isn't the same thing: at least I would try to find parity. Two months wasn't so bad and I liked Kirstie and she liked me. Her grandmother had just died of Alzheimer's and she wanted to help old people. She was on my course at college. Kirstie thought Baxter's work was freaky. I said it had to be worth trying. We couldn't give up.

Kirstie said we'd had our time and like the dinosaurs, time was up. She wasn't being funny.

I didn't agree but many thought like Kirstie. We had a death wish, a fatalism. Mortality is a strange thing. We learn at a young age that death is inevitable, yet how many of us meet our mortality only late in life when memory is older than the years to come.

$$\Omega$$

Kit: This is Marathias. The harbour is a graveyard of derelicts and wrecks. Following the main channel and watching. Hoping that nothing has sunk and fouled the channel since last I was here. There's a trawler alongside the harbour wall.

I've tied up there before. It's aground and hasn't moved in years. Its hull is a sea of rust and the name's illegible.

My boat is being kind to me. Running forward to drop the fenders over the side. Bumping up against the trawler. Bow rope. Throwing it up over a bollard on the trawlers deck. Secure. My stern's swinging out. Got the boat hook. Using it to hang onto the trawler's rail. It's holding. Gently now. Ease my boat alongside. Good. Stern rope. Tying off. I'm secure.

The sun's going down in a sea of blood red. I'm weary. Need to eat something. Then rest a bit. I said I'd go ashore and say something more about Marathias. Not so sure now. Need to think.

Ω

Kit: Lying down in the fore-cabin. Narrow berth. Kicked off my deck shoes. Not used to being on the boat all day: the constant motion's worn me out. I've eaten something. No way of heating anything and dried fish in cold water is foul, but it's all I have. I've brought no books and I've only a wind-up torch to read by. I'll rest a while.

…

Did you hear that? Wait. Someone's on my boat. Do I mean someone?

…

There it is again. Damn. Torch? Got it. There's nothing to steal on deck. Everything is in here, where it'll keep dry. Why am I whispering? Noise would be better. HEY!

…

I'm winding the torch and at the door. Ready, One!

Swinging the light across the boat. Something there. It's a dog. Two eyes staring in the torchlight.

Hey!

Frightened it off. Leapt back onto the trawler and away. Shame.

Do I mean that? No use for a dog. Dogs die too quickly. But more companionable than a parrot. Can't take a parrot for a walk. Odd, I never think of Wendy. Wendy isn't company, not as such. A dog now.

I scared it off. And I've nothing to feed it with so it has no use for me. But what does it find in Marathias?

The boat's shifting under my feet. Must be a swell. Fenders juddering against the trawler. Sky's clouded over. Pray it isn't bad weather. Pray to what? No one believes any more.

Damn this. I need to sleep. Need to stop talking. Goodnight, friend.

Transcript 012

Kit: My father fell ill quite suddenly, though perhaps we'd been waiting for it ever since his first brush with cancer. I had turned twenty and was halfway through my degree in Gerontics. My knowledge of geriatric care was distant, remote: I knew systems and computer programs, but I didn't know how to care. I didn't even know, if I discount Miss Bramble, what it was to lose a loved one.

I drove down the M4 to my parents' house. There were no lights on the roads. Mama had argued against me driving so far at night, but I'd found the courage to ignore her.

Soon as I was in her house I asked how father was. Mama ushered me into the front room. She seemed smaller, more bird-like than when I had last seen her. She said he was in bed. I wanted to see him. He was sleeping. Mama said he needed to sleep.

I had driven through the night against Mama's wishes. She would make me wait till daylight to see Papa.

I asked about the hospital and a shadow passed over Mama's face before her mouth straightened. She said they'd given him six months, but that doctors knew nothing. I asked if he was in pain. She said he'd always wanted me to succeed.

I was doing okay at college. The economies of death were always on my side. It wasn't enough. I was born special but no one told me how to live up to it. I didn't need a job; fame had brought wealth. But I wanted to be employed because I had nothing better to do, and out of a sense of duty to the human race of which I was the last ever member.

Success is displaced procreation. The Barren made many wealthy.

I slept that night with owls calling in the darkness.

In the morning, house martins flew from the eaves. Papa was awake now. I saw him at breakfast. He was pale but neither he nor Mama spoke of death or cancer. I sensed, only a week after the diagnosis, that normality would rule until the last possible moment.

Papa asked me if I was well. He always called me Kit. Mama always used my full name, Khristos.

I said I was okay. He remarked that I'd driven down the previous night. I said I'd wanted to see him as soon as I could. He leant his head to one side, hiding a mischievous glint in his eye from Mama, and said he was still here. I said we needed to talk, but he shook his head and said we might go for a walk later, if I wasn't too tired from driving.

I said I wasn't tired and would like to walk with him. I glanced at Mama, half-expecting her to intervene. Would she smother him away or abruptly choose to come with us, chaperoning her husband and son? To my surprise she did neither. Time alone with Papa was always brief.

My father and I didn't go far, only into the woods behind the house. Nature, with its continuing growth and rebirth, insulated many from reality. One could believe nothing had changed. But that day, everything had changed. Papa stopped beside a hollow tree and reminded me it was natural to die. Everything did, in the end. I said I knew that, but it wasn't comforting. He smiled and said something about comfort not being the purpose of life. He was more worried for Mama than for himself. I said I'd care for her. He said she wished I lived nearer home. I'd never heard her say that to me.

He didn't want anyone feeling sorry for him. I said I didn't feel sorry for him, so why should anyone else? He knew I was lying. Then father said Mama didn't feel sorry for him either. He surprised me. Papa said Mama only wished to care for him: she was good at caring. Unbearably good.

I didn't stay a second night, though I stayed as long as I could that day. Mama didn't want me driving home in the dark. Papa insisted she allow it. I was a grown man: I could make my own decisions in life.

But driving home late in the dark, I regretted it. Unthinkingly I followed the flash of the road-reflectors and took a slip road off the M4. Heard the sat-nav's warning too late. Stopped and considered backing up but couldn't see if there were CCTV cameras. I didn't want a fine or the hassle. I drove on without knowing if the road was maintained. Road-closures were common, winter damage wasn't repaired and inessential routes were abandoned. Couldn't find a way back to the M4. Road signs were non-existent and the sat-nav's instructions didn't tally with what I could see on the ground. Eventually I pulled over and took the risk of staying in the car overnight. Barely slept. Even then, gangs preyed on anyone who dropped off the patrolled roads. But I heard nothing until birdsong woke me. Turned the car around and retraced my route. Then stopped at a junction to pull bindweed off a road sign.

Money bought good care for my father, but treatment for serious illness hadn't advanced in twenty years: not since the Barren brought other priorities. For him, there was no cure and no remission.

The last time I saw him he made a great effort and climbed from his bed into a wheelchair. I asked where he wanted to go. He said anywhere with people – they were stupid, selfish, prone to tell themselves things that were not and could not be true, yet they were more like him than he was.

Then he asked me if that made sense. I said yes, it did.

I'm telling you this because I'm still in Marathias. The weather deteriorated overnight, as I'd feared it would. The boat would survive the sea but I haven't the stomach for it. Later, I'll give you a tour of the town. What's left of it. But first I need to eat. Dried fish is barely palatable on its own, but it will do; I've no way of heating anything aboard. I've two skinned rabbits with me. Meant to be a gift for Andreas in exchange for salt. I'll go ashore later and make a fire.

I can't talk while chewing fish. Enough.

Transcript 013

Kit: I'm standing in the plateia in the centre of Marathias. It's recognisable, still, though its people would weep to see it. Stucco peeling from the walls like rotten skin. Window frames rotting, or bleached by the sun. When they deported the people to the mainland they left behind everything they couldn't carry. There was no vandalism, just an orderly withdrawal. The glass in the windows is still intact.

Sea is still grim and no sign of it improving. Reconciled to another day and night moored here. Need firewood. Don't want cold food again. Have to scavenge. Contribute to the ruin of Marathias. Make the fire in the *plateia*. I don't like being overlooked and it's open there. The dog last night has me worried. Got a saw with me to cut down anything I find so I can drag it. Walking the street looking for window frames or collapsed roofs. Anything. Dislikeable work. Feel like an intruder. These were people's livelihoods, their homes. Abandoned cars rusting into dust. Let's talk about something else. Anything else.

Between Papa falling ill and his death, there was Joan. She would have married me, had I asked her. I was twenty-two. Almost half the women in the world were of child-bearing age. But there were no children, except in photographs and movies, and the animatronic dolls made in Japan and Korea.

I'd broken my leg in a climbing accident. Joan had taken it on herself to drive me to work each day as they couldn't spare me from the office. She waited for me outside my apartment and phoned me. I took the lift down to her. She was waiting in her car and greeted me. I liked being mothered a little. Mothered, that is, by a woman I wanted to sleep with. It was raining. I remember that. She got wet holding the car door open. She'd driven miles out of her way, but that hadn't registered with me. She passed the crutch inside and closed the door. As she crossed to the driver's side, I quickly fastened the seat belt to prove that I was at least partially capable. I enjoyed her pampering but also resisted it. I knew that if a woman is denied children she will often mother anything that needs caring for. I wanted to enjoy her care but not depend on it. Joan was blonde, round faced, and womanly. I began to look forward to her presence in the morning. When the fibre-sheath came off my leg there seemed no reason not to carry on seeing her.

Found a door. Jemmied it off the hinges. Dragging it back to the *plateia*. Can break it down into planks. Where was I? Joan. We went to see a triple-bill of ancient movies. The Munchkins were played by midgets. Fairground grotesques hired by the studio. Judy Garland hated them and even the dog was better paid. I tried telling this to Joan in the cinema but she said I was spoiling it for her. I tried to watch the screen, but I was unfamiliar with the cinema habit. It was distracting sitting among strangers. Joan was whispering the lines alongside the actors, and I heard others doing the same. It was a triple bill of child stars: Temple, Taylor, and Garland. We'd skipped the first two. *The Wizard of Oz* was Joan's favourite.

When Dorothy returned to Kansas, Joan started to cry. I put my arm around her shoulder. She asked me not to, saying the ending always made her cry. Dorothy had abandoned her dreams for a lifetime of monochrome domesticity on a farm, but that wasn't why Joan was crying. I was glad when the screen faded and the lights came up.

We shuffled out in the crowd. The theatre bar had closed and the elderly attendant was happy to see us all go. Small hours of the morning, the London streets were deserted and through the city lights I could see a few of the brightest stars. I pointed out Orion, The Hunter, but Joan didn't care for the stars. She said they were too far away and meant nothing to her. Maybe she'd never seen them like I had. Or maybe she had and they still meant nothing.

Joan leant against me and I offered to drive her home.

I'm using the jemmy to pull the door to pieces. I'll need more than this for a decent fire, but it's a start. Trying to forget there were once people here. A town. So many lives and now just me, Lord of it all. I am Lord of decay and destruction.

Joan lived in a Camden Town high-rise. Nineteen-seventies design classic, she said. One-time cutting edge, turned slum, turned heritage. Left the car in the basement and took the lift to the fourteenth floor. I can still remember the number of her flat, 1419. She leant against me in the polished steel box of the lift and I held her and watched the floor indicator.

We kissed in the doorway to her flat. She was letting me in to the chaos of her life, though all our lives were chaos, however well we may have hidden it. She pushed me through an inner door and disappeared into a kitchen to make coffee with an instruction I wasn't to touch her plants.

The room was clean, large, and crowded with green leaves, fronds, stems in pots. They were so perfect I thought they were artificial. But when I looked closer I understood.

Mama was unable to keep any house plant alive for more than a few weeks. After shedding most of its leaves the naked stem would yearn for the window light, as though desperate to escape her. Eventually the sickly remains would be removed to the graveyard in our back garden. Only an aspidistra escaped her, feigning death and once abandoned recovering on the rich diet of its decaying predecessors.

But Joan had none of my mother's failings. Here I saw begonias turning their leaves to me like green hearts and cordylines with perfect curving spears. None of the plants leant toward the window and many had a spotlight hanging from the ceiling. I didn't ask if she knew their names as I was sure she could tell me both their common and Linnaean classification from cultivar to phylum, in the same way a mother could tell you everything about her children.

Joan was watching me. I said they were extraordinary and admired her skills. She said she was allergic to cats. Happily, there were no plants around her bed.

I was never at ease in Joan's apartment. I knew we wouldn't last. Hadn't wanted it to last. Life was transient. I accepted that but I'm not sure Joan did. Not then anyway. Maybe later she did.

Perhaps I was harsh, too unaccepting. There were more extreme ways women bereft of children sought to escape. It's hard to imagine one's life any differently, even now, faced with a pile of wood outside an abandoned taverna.

The only thing flourishing here is the bougainvillea. I suppose it was once the taverna owner's pride, a magnificent pink flowering rambler. Now it has taken over, clambering over the roof and around the iron railings of the terrace; smothering it in a spider's embrace.

It reminds me too much of Joan's apartment. I wish I'd chosen somewhere else to make a fire.

Run out of talking for now, but need more wood. Don't want to justify myself any more.

Ω

Kit: It's night. The fire's burning and the rabbit's cooking on the spit. Found everything I needed in the taverna. Worried the smell of rabbit will attract dogs. Keeping a piece of firewood to hand so I've something to protect myself. Should get my gun from the boat but it's too much effort. Besides, that would mean leaving my dinner unattended.

Transcript 014

Kit: Thank God but I'm sailing again. Last night I threw scraps of rabbit to the dog but it didn't come near me. There isn't time to re-domesticate the dog. For all our centuries of careful breeding, in twenty generations all feral dogs will resemble their wild cousins.

But this morning I don't give a damn for eternity. Sea's still filthy from yesterday's weather and the boat ploughs into the waves, but the wind is steady and I have a use for you, my friend. Recall my saying that this Com-Tech recorder uploads my voice to a satellite? Well, the same gives me my bearings. I've my position and my course: Heisenberg would envy me.

I might be young again and I haven't felt a week less than my age in many months. Even my shoulder is uncomplaining. True, tomorrow I'll feel older for nursing my pains, but not now. Now I sail.

So Joan? Yes, done with Joan for now. Saw her once or twice after *The Wizard of Oz* but we were drifting. I took up running. Maybe in my work I saw death too near and wanted something to hold it back. How morbid at twenty-two to worry about mortality. Many were living an eternal youth of plastic surgery and hair transplants.

After Joan then. Well, Joan did return, but that was years later. Another time for that story. But after Joan and I split up, my father died. Yes, that's what happened next. Can't talk of that now. Not while sailing. Need time to reflect. So, Daniel. Daniel with the plastic sister? I met him again. It was not long after my father's funeral. I'll come back to the funeral when I've landed. In peace and quiet.

Wait. Need to bring in the foresail. Carrying too much wind.

…

That's better. It was forcing the bow down into the waves. Well, now Daniel was a face in the office. I thought there would be several of us in the bar after work, but it was just us two in the crowds. I didn't go out late after work, not as a habit, but invites are hard to ignore at Christmas. I asked where everyone else had got to. Daniel didn't know. He didn't want to be there. At least, no more than I did. Entertainment and social gatherings had a false jollity, as I imagine they did in wartime. Only no war had gone on this long. A band played old Christmas songs, each sounding like the last. I didn't recognise most of them. Each Christmas was a repeat of the last, as though it was on hold until there was a cause for celebration. I wondered if Papa had known the same songs. I doubted Mama would recognise any. This year there was no avoiding the holiday at my parents' house. It would be strange without Papa but I couldn't leave Mama on her own.

Daniel was unhappy. I thought he was bothered by the band, but it wasn't that. It was everything. He spread his hands and said the whole world, the whole fucking world was messed up. He said God was testing us, see. God wanted us to see how bad we'd made everything.

I said that whatever sense God might once have meant to me I had long ago lost.

Daniel looked at me; I mean, really looked, as though seeing me for the first time. He couldn't understand why I had no belief. Me, of all people, the *Last-Born Man*.

I didn't want to talk about God in the pub. I said my birth was a long time ago. He looked stunned, as though he'd opened a present and found it empty. I'd disappointed him, again.

I thought of Hannah and her instinctive optimism. My optimism was more calculated: fate had made me the last-born man and I didn't want that fame. I recall even then, more than twenty years into the Barren, most women were convinced that there would be an answer and one day there would be more children. Men were less certain and less interested. Self was the new family, the new responsibility. Leading a good self was the goal. Men were good at self.

Daniel thought God was testing us. He said there wasn't any other way of understanding it. If it wasn't God, then all we had was science and that had failed to find a cure in over twenty years of trying.

I reminded him of Professor Baxter, but Daniel dismissed him, saying his work was evil and he deserved what he got. So I reminded him I was there the night he died. Daniel looked grim. He said Baxter was just wrong.

I'd worked alongside Daniel for two years and had absolutely no idea what was in his head.

He asked if I prayed. I said I had, once. He wanted to know why I stopped. I said I didn't believe any more.

Then we stopped arguing and he asked how I thought it would end. I said we were making the end. Our work building care facilities was the end. We were building the future, what there remained of it, the industrialisation of geriatric care, turning nursing into a process. How else might we cope with a population of the aged and incapable and none left to care for them?

Daniel swore that wasn't for him. Not those "death houses". He wanted to know what I'd choose. I said I wouldn't need to choose until much later. He remembered I had money. I had choices.

Yes, I admitted it made a difference, though not as much as he supposed. Never known what it was to be like everyone else. It fucks you up a bit.

It was obvious Daniel didn't want me there, so I said I was leaving. Then Daniel was all apologetic so I sat down again. It was just Christmas, he said. We were, ironically, celebrating a birth.

He drank and the way he drank told me his beer would be the first of many. I wouldn't stay and watch.

I asked how he would end it. Pill or injection, he said. Or gas. He thought there'd be a poison gas. Something giving instant painless death, but it wouldn't be suicide. Euthanasia, more like. Everyone would do it.

Three of our colleagues joined us and we spoke of troubles at work: the difficulty of getting construction supplies, how long we could rely on African labour. The conversation bored me and I left early.

Daniel left the company the following March. I've no idea where he went or what happened to him afterwards. I hope he got what he was looking for.

I'll stop talking now. That Christmas seems so far away; two-thirds of a lifetime and many kilometres. If you don't mind I want to be alone for a while.

$$\Omega$$

Kit: The back of my neck has caught the sun but I'm in the lee of Andreas's island. Another mile and I can drop anchor. His place is a half kilometre inland. He says the sea keeps him awake. Cold food tonight. I'll drop anchor and go ashore in the morning. Not safe to land tonight. It will be dark soon.

Transcript 015

Kit: Why not now? I don't need a light to talk by. Wait; I'll not begin yet. I'm bone-weary and my head is soft from too much wind and sun. Lying in the fore-cabin and not falling asleep. Wait a moment.

...

That's better. Sitting on deck. The night's cool but I'd rather sit under the stars.

...

Sorry. I was shivering. Went for a blanket. Wrapped up now. Want to talk about my father's death and funeral. Not been looking forward to recalling this. Been re-reading his letters in the days leading up to now. They're safe at home, in Wendy's care. I'm serious. If there's a fire he knows what to save from the house and Papa's letters are among them.

My father wrote every day in his last months. Much of it was nonsense because the drugs made him delirious. But some of it burns with clarity. He wanted me to know that he loved me and that he loved my mother. Why are people condemned to say what others already know; what they've spent their lives proving? I've read them so many times that the words have fractured in the folds of paper and I read half from memory.

My father died at home, in his sleep. A sleep aided by painkillers. Don't know if he deliberately overdosed and it didn't matter to me if he did, though Mama would care. Her religious beliefs burned underground most of her life, so far as I knew her life, but would flare up in a crisis.

The cremation was very English. My father would have approved. Mama wore black of course, every inch of her the Greek widow and dramatic as a black swan. I did not wear black. Mourning had become unfashionable. I wore the same suit I'd wear to an interview. Mama did enough grieving for both of us. I grieved like the Englishman I was. That occasion was also the last time I saw my father's parents. A year later they booked themselves onto a cruise ship and didn't come back. 'Gone abroad' took on a new meaning in those years. Can't blame them. I'd seen the future. Even helped build some of it.

The church service was on a warm spring day. Crocuses were in flower, and white bunches of snowdrops. That winter had been mild and full of rain. I came out of the chapel having touched Papa's coffin one last time and in the garden of remembrance I stared at the ground and cried. Mama found me and pressed her hand in mine. It was a rare show of affection. I think she recognised that even if I didn't wear black I carried it on the inside. I grieved for Papa. I still grieve for Papa.

Mama moved to Greece the year after. First Athens, then when it grew too dangerous, out to the village where she grew up. She had extended family there. She practised her grief as the old folk died off. I suppose it was then I thought about not staying in England, or at least thought about where I would eventually go to die. I had no intention of building my own mechanical tomb. Call me a hypocrite, but money has its blessings.

Should get some sleep soon. I hope Andreas will be happy to see me. It's hard sometimes when you're used to being alone to share space and time with another. He might tell you something about his life. I should like that. This can't all be about me, can it?

The stars are wonderful tonight. I don't look at them often enough. The patterns in the stars have endured across all of man's history. How many things can say that?

Mama died ten years ago. She made life hell for her carer. The woman was a Somali, grateful for the pay. She sent half of it home to her relatives. Don't know what happened to her after Mama died. I have a photograph of Mama's grave. Couldn't get to the funeral. Transport in Greece collapsed years ago, the roads crumbling, railways abandoned. Greece had been the poor man of Europe for decades. Hadn't the resources to cope when things got bad. I knew the date and time of the service and tried to join in via vid-cam but I couldn't see who was talking and didn't know what I was supposed to do.

Wanted to give Mama's house to the Somali woman but she didn't want it. She wanted another rich old Greek to care for so she could send money home. I gave her 20,000 dollars. The house is in my name now, but there's no one to buy it. I'm getting ahead of myself. Need to slow down. I'll talk more tomorrow.

Not seen a light ashore. Can see Andreas's place from here, but no light's showing. Perhaps he had an early night. Best not to think of any other reason an old man's light mightn't show. Nothing I can do anyhow, floating under the Milky Way.

How does the poem go? *No man is an island entire to himself*, something like that.

Transcript 016

Kit, auto-translated from Greek: Say again.

    Unidentified human male: Say what?

    Kit: About this.

    Unidentified human male: Is that thing recording me? I don't want it.

    Kit: Does it bother you?

    Acquiring voice profile.

    Unidentified human male: Why do you want to record me?

    Kit: I'm not recording you. I'm recording me.

    Unidentified human male: What the hell for? Switch it off. Damn you, Zachariades. Let me be.

    Kit: I thought you were dying.

Unidentified human male: I am dying. Switch it off and leave me alone. We're all dying.

Kit: You can't be like this.

Unidentified human male: Why not?

Kit: Because, Andreas, you'll die.

Voice profile acquired. Identified as Andreas Alexandris. Tagged as Andreas.

Andreas: Ha! We will all die. This is it: you and I and the other old folks. We are fossils; we just do not know it.

Kit: I need salt.

Andreas: Take it. What do I care?

Ω

Kit: It's not so simple. A saltpan works by allowing sea water into a shallow basin and then damming it so the water cannot escape. As the sun evaporates the trapped water, the salt crystallises out and floats on the surface in rafts of glistening white. The edge of the lagoon here is a low ridge of earth and stone. The sea's broken it down, so I'm re-laying stones and packing them with earth. It's more work than I expected. Days of work.

You wonder why I haven't built a saltpan of my own. Well, I have. Three times. It's not so easy.

How long has Andreas been like this? When I found him I thought he was dying, or near death; instead, he was drunk. I think he has given up. He was once so proud of his independence here. Andreas stays sober today, at least. I made him promise me that.

Didn't record anything yesterday. Didn't seem like a good time. Also, Andreas gets angry when I'm talking into the recorder. I'm talking now because I'm on my own. Sun's glaring off the water. Hurts my eyes. Salt water is chafing my hands. If I seem breathless, forgive me.

Wanted to say more about Mama. She wore black for six months after papa's funeral. Excessive? She thought not. It was then she spoke of returning to Greece. I told her the Greek economy was broken. She did go back, for six months, then returned to north London and nothing more was said. She went to Papa's grave, to where his ashes were scattered, once a week for I can't remember how long. Her hair was still dark. She still had her figure. She hadn't grown fat, like so many Greek women do. She had suitors; there was money in the bank so I couldn't blame them. She teased me, saying she would marry one of them and spend my inheritance. I said I didn't care, though I was lying.

I think she went back to Greece to avoid all those men. I got a call telling me she was going and I was to drive her to Heathrow. That was it: no dissuading her this time.

Andreas: They say it is the first sign of insanity.

Kit: Morning. Didn't know you were about.

Andreas: I get around. A storm broke it.

Kit: So I see.

Andreas: More than I could do to fix it up.

Kit: This is hard work. You're a decade older than me.

Andreas: Are you telling me how old I am or telling that machine?

Kit: Both. We all talk to ourselves. Even my parrot talks to itself.

Andreas: Does that robot?

Kit: Wendy isn't human.

Andreas: Neither is your parrot. A robot would be useful here, do what you're doing.

Kit: I couldn't risk him doing this.

Andreas: No?

Kit: Salt is corrosive. Salt water even more so.

Andreas: Not waterproof? Ha! What happens when it rains?

Kit: He takes shelter, like you or I. He, it, is old: had it ten years. Can't be sure… it does stuff, just not this.

Andreas: You should live here.

Kit: With you?

Andreas: You can tend my grave when I am gone. I want to be buried on that hill.

Kit: How far is it?

Andreas: A kilometre, maybe. You do it? Exchange for salt.

Kit: Is that the bargain?

Andreas: It is.

Kit: Then I've no choice. I need salt.

Andreas: Do not worry about digging a grave. Soil too damn thin. Roll stones over me.

Kit: You'll have a proper grave, unlike me. I expect to lie where I fall.

Andreas: But you should think about living here. You come for salt and there's everything here that you have where you are. Besides, I'll need someone to haunt.

Kit: That was funny. I need a rest. As you say, this is hard work. This recorder. I'm telling it my life, from birth to now.

Andreas: So you said. You think I do not remember but I do.

Kit: You heard me telling it my mother returned to Greece after my father died.

Andreas: Why did she do that? She had everything where she was. Greece was ruined.

Kit: Guess she didn't have everything she wanted.

Andreas: You did not argue against it.

Kit: First time she wanted to live in Greece, yes. She tried but went back to London. Second time – you know what mothers are like. Hard to argue with them.

Andreas: True. My father the same. Always arguing with him. I tell him the world is changing and his advice no longer true. Would not listen.

Kit: Yet we miss them.

Andreas: I miss my brothers more.

Kit: You should stay with me for a while. You aren't doing so well.

Andreas: Ach.

Kit: I'm serious.

Andreas: You cannot stay here?

Kit: Repairs. Damage to my roof. And the olives to harvest. Things don't wait. I'll stay here only long enough to repair this and gather salt.

Andreas: That hill up there.

Kit: I promise. I'll bury you on that hill.

Andreas: And I promise to think about coming with you when you leave. Now turn that thing off. It does not need to hear us.

$$\Omega$$

Kit: Stretching my back. God I'm stiff. Andreas has gone back up to his house. Worried about him. When I said I had to leave soon he clasped his head in his hands. Thought he was going to cry. Kept picking bits of earth and breaking them in his fingers. He could be dead, easily, in six months. Seeing myself in him in I don't want to think how many years.

All those years designing factories to avoid the need for one human to wait upon another as they die. Where now are my wonderful machines?

Transcript 017

Kit: I remember driving Mama to the airport the day she flew out to Greece. The roads were busy and we'd set off early. Ridiculously early.

Mama said I was too cautious, like my father. She often compared me unfavourably to Papa. In fact, the car fought against the fuel-saving fifty-limit. It wanted to be off the leash.

I said our speed was no different to most, but that wasn't wholly true. The fifty-limit was only nominally observed and despite the surveillance cameras, few were ever prosecuted. But my birthright kept me newsworthy and I'd grown up with the habit of not getting noticed. I followed laws to the letter.

Mama gestured as an articulated pulled out, smoke belching, and surged past. The car swayed.

I said we wouldn't be late. Mama said, if we were, she'd wait and get another ticket. She thought I wanted to sabotage her going. Not true. The same reasons against were still there, what with the Greek economy and a population ageing faster than any other nation in Europe. But Mama had family in Greece. A sister and an aunt: she'd lost her parents a few years earlier. In England she only had me and my father's relatives and when they put up no argument against her going, perhaps I worried responsibility for Mama would fall wholly onto me. Selfishly, I thought this was for the best. Had I known that claustrophobic drive would be the last time I would see my mother, other than on a vid-cam screen, would I have said or done anything different? Would she?

Mama reminded me again to visit Papa's grave and look after it. I promised I would. I got agency workers to do the groundwork. The crematorium was always short-staffed. Mostly migrant workers. Intended to call on Papa once a month, but it was too weird standing beside a tree and trying to connect it with my father.

Wish I had his letters with me now. I re-read them often, at least once a year, but now I want to read them I can't. Another time. It's late and I'm tired. I'm hoping Andreas is asleep.

Andreas: Well, I am not. What are you sitting there for? Talking to yourself, as if I did not know.

Kit: I was saying goodbye to my mother.

Andreas: Eh?

Kit: No matter. You're not asleep, then.

Andreas: I could not.

Kit: Why?

Andreas: For you wandering around out here. I am not used to company.

Kit: I was sitting.

Andreas: Same thing. Do not argue. Why you always cross me?

Kit: I didn't know I was.

Andreas: Well, now you know.

Kit: It's dark. I can't see Andreas, but I think he's standing in the door. The recorder shows a red light when it's on so I know he can see me.

Andreas: You speaking to me or that thing?

Kit: To the recorder. I was describing here and now. Look, I've forgotten how to talk, except to tell Wendy what to do or to amuse the parrot.

Andreas: Do not believe that. You have talked enough today. God, it runs out of you. Know why you speak into that thing?

Kit: Yes.

Andreas: Why, then?

Kit: Because I hope one day someone will listen.

Andreas: So, you understand.

Kit: I think so. Help me up. My legs are stiff. I'm younger than you, but not so young.

Andreas: Here. My hand. Wait till you're my age. If you make it so far.

Kit: Thank you. I'll just lean against the tree a bit. You've been drinking. Can smell it on you.

Andreas: Two glasses. Two only. Do I seem drunk?

Kit: No.

Andreas: Now you have a glass with me, be civilised. But turn that thing off first.

$$\Omega$$

Kit: Been listening back to all that. Don't recall much of last night. Drank more than one glass. Looking over what I managed yesterday I'm surprised I got so much done. Think I can rebuild the wall and make the pan secure in a day or so. Day after I'll let the sea in and the day after maybe harvest the salt.

Hands are a mess. Rubbed olive oil on them last night, but the salt has cracked the skin of my knuckles. Feels raw. Stones are hard on my hands.

Might get breathless talking and heaving stones, but I'll try. Mama and I arrived early at Heathrow and had to wait two hours for them to call her flight. Two of the five terminals were disused but I was surprised so many still flew; prices were astronomical compared to twenty years before. Then we got a call saying her flight would be delayed an hour while they fixed a fault. Three hours is a long time to say goodbye.

Mama wanted to know I would visit her. She reminded me Greece was my country too.

Of course, I said I would. Wasn't conscious it was a lie, but it proved one. Tried to convince her it was okay. Said there were practical reasons not to live in Greece, but she would be happier there with her family.

In that one sentence I said more to her than I'd said all day. She stared at me a moment, then shrugged and asked if I imagined she ever intended being sad. She'd mourned Papa, paid her respects. I misunderstood and thought she intended to remarry.

She was not. She had no intention of remarrying. She had all she needed and silly men only amused her. Not one of them, she said, was a match for my father. It had amused her to see how anxious they were. An old woman enjoys the flattery.

I said she wasn't so old.

Faced with departure, we were dropping our guard.

Hope you let them down gently, I said.

Mama said she was never cruel to them. No more cruel than they, chasing a widow for her money.

Flattery is a dubious currency, but if it made her happier then who am I to judge?

I'm smiling one of those stupid smiles as I'm remembering it. I told Mama, No one ever talked to me the way you did. She answered, No other laboured for thirty hours to bring you into the world.

And it nearly killed you, I said.

She asked me again to visit her, so she could go on talking to me like no other. It's true; no one ever spoke to me like Mama.

This is maudlin. I need marching bands. Communist work-songs. Don't think Andreas will oblige. Ach. Silence is better than hearing me yacking.

$$\Omega$$

Kit: You like watching me work?

Andreas: It is a novelty to see work not done with my own hands. That robot, what did it cost?

Kit: 700,000 Euros. Why do you ask?

Andreas: That is a great deal.

Kit: I had the money and it wasn't doing me any good sitting in a bank. I wanted to live, and live as well as I could. Is that a crime?

Andreas: No, but nor is it just.

Kit: No, it's not just, but I don't see the benefit of it now, labouring up to my knees in saltwater. There.

Dropped another stone in position. Packing mud around it to seal the joints.

Andreas: You shall have it done tomorrow.

Kit: Tonight, I hope. Tomorrow I let the water in and dam it.

Andreas: It will rain tomorrow.

Kit: You think?

Andreas: Or tonight. I am used to this place.

Kit: You can tell only by the sky?

Andreas: Mostly. See that haze? It could mean rain, I cannot be sure.

Kit: I hope you're wrong. At least it's cooler today.

Andreas: I brought water. I thought you might be thirsty.

Transcript 018

Kit: I didn't finish yesterday. Perhaps I was distracted by Andreas's warning – he was right: it's raining and the sky is grey. Of course, it may have been that while my mind was willing, my body was not. Not worked this hard in a long time.

Even if I had finished yesterday, the weather would have stopped the pan evaporating, so I'd still need another day. The rain is cooling the air and though I'm wet through, work is easier this morning. There's another advantage: Andreas is inside, out of the weather so I can talk as much as I wish. Hear that, Andreas? I'm talking as much as I like! Sometime I'll get Andreas to talk to you about his life, but so far he's refused.

Mama was happier in Greece than she'd been in London. Leastways, I thought she was happier: how does one tell? She called at least once a week, always with her sitting out on a veranda, blue sky behind her, sunglasses on. I was all set to fly out one Christmas when the ban on non-essential flights came in. Fuel saving, they called it, but it was as much to curb immigration. I tried to get work contracts in Greece. I had an excuse that business travel was classed as essential, but the Greeks had no money for expensive geriatric facilities. Instead, like my mother did, most employed East African migrant carers while a few adventurous souls hitched a berth aboard cargo ships to satisfy their world-lust. Maybe I was never adventurous enough.

Talking to Mama became like answering a census form, which we filled in every two years. They had been once a decade, but with demographics changing so rapidly data had to be updated.

I was twenty-seven, single, my father dead, my mother two-thousand kilometres away in Greece. Work became my focus: for a time I genuinely believed automation offered a painless and dignified old age. GeriCo's central offices were near Oxford. I was a consultant designer. Most of the contracts were from central and local government in the UK and Europe. Interest from the US a couple of times but the hi-tech solutions we offered couldn't compete with Mexican and Central American labour. GeriCo was desperate to get into the

Chinese market: after thirty years of the one-child policy their population crisis rivalled anywhere in the world, but they had their own way of dealing with that.

Mostly I remember the hours of driving and shaking hands with strangers. They'd show me local demographic forecasts. Give me a tour of possible development sites. I'd set up a video-link with one of our prime geropolises – that's a city of the old – usually Windsor or Grantham, and the client would see what we offered: comfortable, dignified, high-tech, socially-independent geriatric care. Christ. You can only live a lie for so long. The lie ended in Worcester when the River Severn had its worst floods in sixty years.

I remember the press pack waiting for us at the entrance. The GeriCo entourage were like penitents waiting for their scourging. The most senior of us was Ms Stenson. Tall. Blonde. Professional. She truly believed the GeriCo ethos. I was at the lowest end of the pecking order, there only to take note of what had failed and design better next time.

The press pack focused on Stenson. Wanting to know who was to blame. She said no one was to blame, and we would ensure this would never happen again.

They wanted a figure for the number of deaths. We didn't have the information yet. There'd be a press release later.

Then one of them saw me and called my name. She asked why the facility had been built on a known flood zone. I said she'd have to take that up with local planning. They gave us permission to build.

Another journalist called me. Stenson was irritated I was getting too much attention, but I couldn't avoid answering this question: Did I regret being the last-born man?

Strange that even there, among so much death, my little fame attracted attention. I fobbed him off, saying I regretted none were born after me.

Then we got past the press and into what had been the atrium. Huge glass walls. The air-con was down and the sun had warmed the air. Rescue services had cleared the complex, but the smell of death remained.

Stenson approached and congratulated me on my handling of the journalist. She thought it strange someone could be the centre of interest without having done anything to merit it.

I often thought the same.

Stenson was regional manager: regional being the UK and most of France. Our visit wasn't to learn lessons: the lessons were blindingly obvious. Planning had chosen the site, not GeriCo. We'd built as they advised. I thought I knew what to expect from the news reports but the smell coming from the lower floors crept under my assumptions. Before descending, we put on hazard suits. We changed quickly, Stenson and another woman member donning their gear in a side office. The rest of us changed in the atrium. The suits had a breather pack. Then site security took us down the escalators. Stenson was flanked by her team. I was on the edge of it, nearest the unit manager who had the look of a man awaiting execution.

The higher wards were unaffected, save that electrical failures had shut down the medical equipment. Those on dialysis or ventilation had died in their beds. Several other residents had seen the staff fleeing and collapsed of shock. But that was nothing compared to the devastation on the lower wards. Standard height for a ward bed was point six-five metres to give the droids access. All that we could see in the gloom were the skeletal remains of bed frames and piles of mattresses. The surge had smashed most of the windows and broken glass gleamed in the mud. At least they let in air and light. The flood defences failed at 3am, when the residents were in bed. Left a slick mark at one-point-one metres around the ward. Five members of staff died. Twenty residents somehow got out alive. The mud clogged our boots until we could barely walk.

...

I'm up to my shins in salt water but the brine smells better than those drowned wards. If you don't mind, I'll sit for a while. Enough talking.

Transcript 019

Kit: Worcester. Haven't done with that memory, grim though it was. We were halfway through the ward when Stenson stopped at one of the bed frames. The mattress had gone, along with the patient. Bed restraints hung either side of the frame.

She asked the manager if the patients were restrained in bed. They were. Not enough staff to supervise all the wards. Many residents had some form of dementia. It was for their safety.

Through his bio hood, the manager's voice barely rose above a whisper. The green emergency lighting didn't penetrate the shadows at the end of the ward.

Stenson asked me for the ward capacity. I recall it was two-hundred and twelve, five thousand in the whole unit. I guessed it was running at ninety-three percent occupancy. The manager corrected me; it was ninety-eight percent. Two hundred and eight in this ward accounted for. Twenty survivors. Five hundred and seventy-two known casualties. Fifteen missing.

Two of the upper wards served as temporary morgues. New refrigeration units were on their way.

The shadows at the edges of the room seemed deeper. Stenson had barely moved from the central aisle where the light was brightest. When she said we'd seen enough, no one objected.

Back on the escalator Stenson removed the hood of her suit and gestured for us to do the same. The stench hung in the air and now we'd seen the wards it seemed even more oppressive. The unit manager followed a few metres behind. Security followed him. Stenson touched my arm and asked if this was my first experience of disaster management. It was my second, but the first major one. She asked what we'd learned. Wanted to say I would devote myself to poetry or anything that removed me from this horror. The process fails, the machine fails. GeriCo and the other geriatric care providers sold a lie: there was no comfortable death. Instead, I said we'd learnt that the site failed through a failure of flood defences; something we had no control over.

Stenson agreed, but went further. GeriCo must be wholly autonomous. Society would inevitably fail; therefore GeriCo couldn't depend on society.

Gerontics, she said as we climbed the motionless escalator, was the only thing that mattered and it must be free to monitor itself, for the benefit of all.

I doubted very much if Ms Stenson or any in her team imagined somewhere like Worcester would be their last home. I knew it wouldn't be mine. Six months later I handed in my notice. Later, I wrote letters and articles challenging the power of GeriCo and care providers, but it was too late: even before I left, I knew that we'd done everything to ensure that GeriCo had government in its pocket. Geriatric costs terrified those still young enough to enjoy their money. In the long run, droids cost less than human labour and would never need carers of their own.

So my career ended and now I find I've talked my way into finishing the dyke. Walking back towards Andreas's house. Tomorrow, if the rain has stopped, I can start to make salt. Wet through. Taking my shirt off to wring it out. Rain's cold on my back. Got a change of clothes inside and the rest of the day to fill. Glad to be standing upright again. Horizon's brightening. Better weather, I hope. Get inside out of this. Andreas is sleeping.

Andreas: I was sleeping, until I heard you muttering to yourself. You have finished?

Kit: Yes. You were right about the rain. I think it's brightening up. What does your weather sense say about tomorrow?

Andreas: Cannot see the sky from here.

Kit: I need dry clothes.

Andreas: Don't mind me. Want some bread?

Kit: Is it good?

Andreas: It's hard on the teeth, but not bad.

Kit: He's piling it on a plate.

Andreas: I hear you. You're talking as if I'm not here.

Kit: I'm recording, yes. Just saying what's happening.

Andreas: It should come with video.

Kit: It can't handle that much data.

Andreas: Tell me, why you never marry?

Kit: Didn't know you were interested in my life.

Andreas: You're the only other here. Whose life should I take an interest in? I have nothing to say to myself, but you, you never stop. So, why you never marry?

Kit: Didn't seem any point.

Andreas: True, true. No reasons to marry if there are no children, for children are the point of marriage. But *I* married, many married. Did we all think that somehow, by a miracle, he Joseph, she Mary, they would bear a child?

Kit: But you married for love and love is blind, so they used to say.

Andreas: I *still* say. Yes, I loved my Elena. I love her still.

Kit: Maybe I never found someone I loved enough. The bread is hard, as you say. It's slow eating.

Andreas: Or you were not so lovable, Zachariades. You are – what is the phrase? Above others?

Kit: He's gone out to shake the crumbs from the board. You're wrong, Andreas. I don't think I'm better than anyone.

Andreas: No, not better, but you are distant, never really here. A hard man to know. I give you my island, but I'm not so sure I even like you.

Kit: We're neighbours, isn't that enough?

Andreas: Perhaps. And you promise to bury me.

Kit: Yes. But you'd better show me where.

Andreas: Come! Come, then!

Kit: Now?

Andreas: I may drop dead this moment, and then what? Come, bring your food.

Kit: I'm following him outside. The rain has eased. He's staring into the hills, a hand above his eyes.

Andreas: Up there on that ridge. You see that tall pine?

Kit: Which tall pine?

Andreas: That one. Are you blind?

Kit: I don't see. No... now I do. I'll bury you under the tall pine. From there, can you see across the island?

Andreas: Why you ask?

Kit: I'd like to see the island.

Andreas: It has everything a man needs, including salt.

Kit: I'd still like to look over the island. It doesn't seem so high.

Andreas: You are crazy. But I will not keep you. No, not from that ridge. Go beyond it. Follow the track as far as the olive grove, you want to see the trees, see if my olives are worth picking. Then follow the goat paths until you reach the top. See whole island from that hill. I climbed it, many times.

Kit: You need to decide what you want to take with you. I mean, if you're returning with me. Remember, it all has to go on the boat.

Andreas: Ay, ay. I know. I have thought about it, and you are right. Your offer is kind and I am indebted. No man should be alone too long. There was a woman, you know. I have not seen her in a while.

Kit: A woman?

Andreas: My other neighbour.

Kit: Here, on this island?

Andreas: No, she is like you: keeps to herself. Kyrios. She lives on Kyrios. You can see it from up there. Now go. Leave me to say my goodbyes.

…

Kit: I'm walking away. Andreas has gone back to his house. I'm recalling a poem. Something about Cortez standing on a peak in Darien to see an ocean.

There's no pine tree taller than any other. Andreas's sight is failing.

Transcript 020

Kit: I have water. Andreas assured me there are no springs or useable wells between his place and the hill. Assume he's right. It's warm, but not uncomfortably so and there's a wind. Stopping every hundred metres to make sure I can recognise the coast behind me. Not easy to see the path and I don't want to lose my way. Climbing up the old terraces that once divided the fields. The stones have tumbled. Hoping for some shade along the way. Can see a stand of walnut and Turkey oaks away to the right but can't tell the extent. Keep going up. Can't be far. Think I can walk and talk without getting breathless.

I wasn't the only one to leave GeriCo after Worcester. Had the unit manager killed himself, I wouldn't have been surprised: he looked a shadow when we left him that day. Instead, he took holy orders and became a monk. For all I know, he's still a monk. Seemed a joke at the time. Had to wait thirty years to realise the joke was on me. I've become a monk, albeit without holiness or belief. No, not a monk: a hermit, a wise fool. I had my own brush with belief after leaving GeriCo, but more of that later.

It was also the first time I got to know Chloe. After touring the Worcester complex, we all stayed in the hotel we'd booked for the press conference. The press had gone and it was just our group at dinner. Half the city had a relative in the complex and we had to pay well over the odds to get accommodation. It had been a wretched day. We were all tired and some of us were hungry. I didn't have much of an appetite, except for alcohol.

Jack Regis, head of media relations, thumped the table and demanded to know when we would be served. I don't think there was anyone Jack hadn't got on the wrong side of at some point.

One of Stenson's suits said we should set an example. Show the town we shared their grief. Stenson agreed, saying that they blamed GeriCo for the deaths and tonight we had to wear sackcloth and ashes. She really said that, sackcloth and ashes.

Jack Regis insisted they were in charge of flood defences and it was nothing to do with GeriCo. Stenson ordered him quiet.

Eventually, the kitchen doors parted and trolleys wheeled in. The staff served us in silence. We indicated what we wanted. They couldn't have done more to show how unpopular we were without slitting our necks.

Stenson made everyone wait until the serving staff had gone. Jack had his knife and fork upright like flag poles, when Chloe March, Stenson's PA, said she wanted to say Grace.

Jack went red.

Stenson suggested Grace was a bit old-fashioned. Chloe said it would only be a prayer for the city, and for those who'd died and their families.

I didn't know Chloe was religious. I'm sure Stenson wasn't and Jack Regis had faith only in himself. I swear Stenson glanced toward the kitchen door, weighing up appearances and PR opportunities. Then she agreed but said she should say something as some of us, meaning Jack, might be more willing to listen if it came from her.

Jack gave Chloe a filthy look and the poor girl shrank back into her chair. Dinner stared from the white china. I remember closing my eyes while Stenson prayed but can't remember a word she said, except all prayers are much the same. I joined in on Amen, though I had spent two decades giving it lip-service.

Chloe thanked Ms Stenson and then we ate.

Entreaties always merge. I don't know what Stenson believed in, except the company. For her, it wasn't milking the old for profit: there was a messianic zeal. We would all grow old and while we might not all end up infantilised or dependent on droids, we had to offer an option other than suicide.

…

I can't be maudlin today. I'm weary, but engaged, considering Andreas's offer. It bothers me there are no natural springs. There are plenty on my island: I suspect a different geology. I've reached the edge of an oak spinney and found the remains of a metalled road. I'm following it. Easier walking than the scrub. Can see Andreas's olive grove. Should find his press, be sure it works. Be sure the trees are pruned. But it'll wait. Besides, Andreas may live for years yet. Tomorrow I'll begin harvesting the salt, but there will be a day or half day when I'm waiting for the sun to finish its work. I'll bring paper and pencil and make survey notes. Need to know if there's any sense abandoning my place to live here. Yes it has salt and my island does not: even so, I don't want the upheaval. If Andreas recovers his spirits and health, he can live on here, and I'll stay where I've lived these last years.

The road ends in a courtyard. Only one building still has a roof. I'm trying the door. Shifting a rock that's holding it shut against the weather. Gloom inside. Wait a moment. Ah!

This is luck. One olive press, recently tended. That's one worry dealt with.

I'm following a field boundary up the flank of the hill. There's still high ground between me and the far side.

Where was I?

Jack Regis was twenty years older than me. Paunch-bellied, a smoker and drinker, an epicurean. Enjoy yourself and to hell with the consequences. After dinner the party split up. Stenson wanted us to stay quiet and dignified, preferably in our rooms. Not Jack's style.

My hotel room was oppressive. I stuck it out for two hours, as far from sleep as Venus is from Mars, then told myself that whisky would help me sleep and went down to the bar. Jack was leaning over a vodka bottle.

He saw me and called across the empty room. I said I couldn't sleep.

That, he said, was the story of his life. Then he said that I'd pissed off Stenson earlier and a glass dropped at my elbow.

Macallan, he said. He knew I liked it.

I wanted to know how I'd annoyed Stenson. He said it was nothing I'd done, it was who I was: *the last-born man*.

Asked him to leave off. It was a bore.

But it wasn't to the press, he said. At the complex, that question just for me. Did I regret being the last-born man?

I wanted him to tell me what else I could have done.

Nothing, Jack said. Nothing at all. But they think you've the secret, the answer. Will the last one out please close the door and switch off the light.

So I told Jack about the schoolteacher who killed herself and that the other kids blamed me. Must have mentioned her. Think I did. Trying to tell all this in some sort of order.

So, you were a poor little fucker then and you're not much better now, Jack said, and he laughed, a big rich laugh and offered me a cigar. I was never a smoker, but sometimes I was a social smoker to get along. People smoked to cock a finger at death. An early death appealed to a lot of people.

Jack reckoned I was all right. Deep down all right. We'd get through it. I thought he meant the Barren, but he laughed again, less cheerfully this time, and said he meant life. Nothing else mattered.

...

I'm here. It's not the highest point on the island; that's further north, but there's sea on three sides. Cairn marks the summit and in time-honoured tradition I'm putting a stone on it, marking my future claim, and making my decision. It has olives, walnuts, salt, goats I can tame or set snares for. I could live well here and Andreas's home would serve me well. True, I would have to dismantle some of my equipment and bring it here, but that's feasible. I hope it won't be soon.

Kyrios, the neighbouring island, is a smudge against the western sky. Shielding my eyes I can make out the line of its hills. Andreas didn't tell me the name of the woman there or how often she calls on him. Perhaps, like me, she comes for salt.

Transcript 021

Kit: GeriCo had seemed like a job for life. GeriCo had a pension plan and healthcare. I think what we were doing at GeriCo scared most of us, but the money was good and the job was secure: that meant something. I was lucky not to need any of it.

Chloe March was at my leaving do, six months after Worcester. She asked me what I was going to do next. Write poetry, I said, forgetting that's not career path open to most people. I apologised and asked what she'd rather be doing with her life.

She wanted to look after her grandmother. Social services weren't up to it. She said something about them just waiting for her grandmother to "fucking" die.

Chloe was one of the quietest women I knew. For her to swear was an event. She apologised. I told her it didn't matter. I'd lost my father so understood the pain. She was unsure I understood at all.

She had an innocent, round-cheeked face and blue eyes. Jack Regis had once called her "doll-face" and got a sexual harassment charge. She reminded me fleetingly of that plastic baby I saw aged seven or eight. But there was nothing fake about Chloe and that night while I was saying goodbye to GeriCo, I realised I would miss her.

Agreed, I didn't understand her situation. My father had good care, even if it hadn't saved him. It made his last year more comfortable.

Chloe's grandmother wasn't comfortable. Worse, she hated being a burden on Chloe.

So I did what I always do, I offered to help. Chloe stared at me. Then she asked how I could help. Money, I said, as though it was easy. As though money meant nothing.

Big mistake. She said I tried to be normal, but I was just weird.

Didn't see her again that evening. Next day sat at home staring at the door, I figured out she thought I was trying to buy her. Maybe I was. I can't tell what I was thinking that night. I liked her and she was having a hard time. What was wrong with trying to help? Why does everything in life have to be a transaction?

I'm waiting for the tide to fill the saltpan. Then I'll block off the inlet. Going to be hot today. Full sun. Ideal for this.

Andreas is gathering his things together. Warned him again there's not much room on the boat. Hope he listened. The name of the woman on Kyrios is Maria Vitalis. She's a year older than me and comes to see Andreas twice a year to gather salt and help with the olive harvest. He's upset that he'll miss her this year. I said he should stay here and ask her to help him, but he refused. Elena was the only woman he ever wanted to depend…

Andreas: Do not speak of my wife.

Kit: Sorry. I didn't see you there.

He's come down from the house and is sitting on a wall at the back of the stone jetty.

Andreas: So, you want to change your mind about giving me a home? Or you are hoping I will change mine? That would be easier for you.

Kit: No, not that. But wouldn't most men prefer to be looked after by a woman?

Andreas: I am not most men. Think on that. Besides, you can have this island when I am gone. You will see her then. Maybe you want woman take care of you.

Kit: She's older than me.

Andreas: Everyone is older than you, Zachariades.

Ω

Kit: Andreas has gone back up to the house. I didn't know Maria Vitalis came with the island. I thought to have it to myself. Myself, Wendy, and the parrot. I'm knee deep in salt water, damming the inlet to the saltpan. It will be most of the day before I can skim off any salt. Got the stone in place and packing around it with mud. Need to drop other stones behind it to hold back the water in the pan once the tide's out. It will be days before my hands recover. Skin's ravaged and split. The cut I got on my arm is healing well and my shoulder feels easier. Perhaps all it needed was exercise.

That was a joke.

That will do. Get out of this water and wash myself down.

Don't want to disturb Andreas; he's best left to himself for the moment. I'll sit here a while.

I tried writing poetry after leaving GeriCo. Joked that all the good poets were only famous when they were dead. Not many laughed. Wasn't much good at it. Never found a theme to write about. If all good poetry comes from within, then I had a problem because there was nothing there. Or maybe I didn't like what I found. But I'm talking to you, aren't I? This isn't poetry, but it's something: a story, an elegy of some kind. Maybe this is okay because I doubt anyone will ever hear it. Or if it is ever heard, by then, everything will be long gone. Well, not everything. They say Mt Rushmore will last a few millennia, along with the radioactive isotopes and non-biodegradable plastic.

Haven't written a poem in decades, or wanted to. I performed once. I got a few lines in and realised I'd lost the audience. Compère introduced me as the last-born man and everyone waited for a meditation on death and humanity. As if I'd write that. I'd spent thirty years avoiding it. Read a poem about birds in a forest and everyone in the audience just tried to work out the meaning when the only damn meaning was birds in a fucking forest. There doesn't have to be a meaning: some things just are. Even Chloe thought she'd found a meaning, when all I was doing was offering to help her.

She got in touch not long after I'd left. An email saying Hi and was it okay to talk. I replied and she wrote back apologising, saying she'd made some assumptions and didn't think she'd been fair on me. I said it didn't matter.

I'd no idea if she genuinely thought that, or had decided she'd suffer me for the sake of getting help for her grandmother. I gave her my number and she called later that day, saying she wanted us to meet. Her voice didn't give away anything and I was careful not to think about her motives. I was taken aback when she suggested we go to St Paul's Cathedral.

She picked up on my reaction and reminded me she was a Christian. Said I remembered her wanting to say Grace at Worcester. She didn't want any reminders of Worcester, had nightmares about it. There was a long pause and I thought she was hanging up. There was someone talking indistinctly in the background. Then she was talking to me again, saying it was beautiful in the cathedral and she felt safe and happy there.

I wanted to know what she felt safe from. She said everything, everything in the world. So I agreed we'd go to St Paul's.

Transcript 022

Kit: Arranged to meet Chloe at the fountains in Trafalgar Square. Seemed less awkward than waiting in a cathedral, should either of us be late. Saturday at two. Scanning the crowd, waiting for her. It was warm. The water splashed invitingly. Square's overlooked by the National Gallery and I'd have sooner gone there and not St Paul's. A cathedral was grand but meant nothing to me; art I thought I understood. Red kites circled the square, worrying a few pigeons. Wedding party emerged from St Martin-in-the-Fields and filled up the steps outside while a photographer did his work. Didn't see Chloe till she was next to me. She apologised for being late and smiled, breaking the placid perfection of her face. She had a bag over her shoulder. I stood up, dusted off the seat of my pants, and we walked toward St Paul's. Four hours later I would be dead.

That's an indulgence. If I'm telling this story then I'll tell it the best I can.

Armed myself with a long-handled rake and I'm raking in the salt. The crystals clump together like floes of ice and I'm drawing them to the water's edge. They're piling up in long drifts. The water absorbs the heat of the sun and will evaporate quicker if I keep taking the salt off it. Moving on to the next pan. Wearing a hat to keep off the sun. The heat is murderous today. Andreas says he's got all his stuff together. Last night he barely spoke five words. Reckon he knows he's unlikely to come back here. Correction, he knows I'll keep my promise and bury him here, but he won't see this place again. Told me about some abandoned wells. The winding gear's gone, but he thinks the shafts are sound. Told me of the olives – last year was poor so this year should be good – and that the goats are too intelligent to be snared. Treating me like a son who'll inherit the estate one day. Good to know these things. Not certain I'll live here or stay where I am. Yes, always need salt, but I can sail for years yet. It's not so bad. So, Chloe and St Paul's.

I stared up into the dome like a small boy and said I hadn't been there in years. My father had taken me, maybe when I was ten.

She asked me if I believed in God. I said I didn't. My mother was Greek Orthodox, but I wasn't anything.

She thought I, of all people, would have faith.

I said I didn't feel chosen.

It wasn't the meeting I expected. She seemed distant. Asked if she was okay. She was pale, though it was hard to tell in the gloom of the cathedral. Assumed this was just the continuation of a mild office acquaintance. Hoped it might be something more than that, but was trying not to be obvious.

Chloe said I was special. God had chosen me to be the last-born. I disowned the idea. I had no wish to be special. Not like that anyway. An accident of birth doesn't make anyone special. Unless you're royalty, I suppose.

She insisted. God had chosen me to be last. I was the last man to be born, maybe ever. I said we would climb up to the top of the dome. Recalled the view of the city from up there. I wanted to be out of the place soon as I could. So we climbed the spiral steps. She was quiet for more than halfway. I'd worked out that if one did believe in God then I did have some significance. I tried to compromise. Said I'd spent most of my life trying to forget there was anything special about me. I said something about being with Baxter when he was killed.

She said Jesus had never wanted to be who he was. He wanted to be left alone, to be a carpenter's son. Already figured this would be my one and only date with Chloe. Something had happened to her in the year since Worcester.

Something bad. Climbing the spiral stairs and the echoing walls reminded me of the wards we'd seen.

I told her about my six months since leaving GeriCo. The poetry. Life. Said my mother was in Greece and I was thinking of going out there. Wasn't sure what to do with myself.

Chloe said she left GeriCo a month previous. They'd let her go. I asked why. She was a good worker. Conscientious. She shrugged.

We stepped onto a balcony overlooking the city. Breeze blew her hair across her face and she turned toward me for shelter. I misunderstood and kissed her. She pushed against me. It wasn't right.

It had been two years since I'd stopped seeing Joan. Apart from a few flings when I'd name dropped who I was to get a woman's attention, I'd not had a relationship. There was something vulnerable and attractive about Chloe.

No sooner did we have a view than she wanted to go down again to pray. I protested, but gave in. On the way down she asked me again. She wanted me to believe so much, but I stuck to the truth. My mother believed but I hadn't inherited it from her. My father had converted to her faith and attended her church for appearances, but he never believed either. I had at least been baptised, though never confirmed.

Kept walking down those stairs. At eight, I'd run down them until I was giddy, then fallen and cut my shin. Now they went on forever. Only Chloe wasn't walking besides me anymore. I turned back. She had stopped to get something from her bag. A woman a few metres behind her screamed. Chloe said she was sorry and the rest was a blur of noise and pain.

I've done well today. The salt's damp still but will dry out tomorrow. Few inches of brine in the saltpan but if I try skimming it off the rake will catch in the silt. Don't want muddy salt. Haven't got enough yet, but this will get me through winter. Then again, another day like today and I'll have salt for a year. No immediate rush to return to my island.

My throat gets dry from so much talking.

Transcript 023

Kit: I'm cutting firewood. It's an hour before sunset and we don't have enough for the night. Setting the blocks on end and quartering them with the axe.

…

Wood is bone-dry. I need to sharpen the axe head.

…

I came-to in hospital. Tubes in my mouth, wires on my chest. Lay there while the anaesthetic wore off. Felt like death. Painkillers did their job, but left an absence of feeling in my middle. In my confused state I was convinced someone had shot Chloe and me. Asked someone if she was okay. Press got hold of that. Reported it as "victim asks after would-be murderer's happiness." Suppose a nurse or porter got a little bonus for the story.

The following day I'd figured out most of what had happened. My surgeon came and shook my hand, saying I'd brought a crowd with me. I'd no idea what he meant, but there was a crowd outside holding a vigil for me. Press release said I was out of immediate danger. Wasn't sure what that meant, so the surgeon warned of infection risks. They'd know in the next day or so. He said Chloe had done me some serious damage and I wouldn't be getting about for a while. Given I had the vitality of a gutted fish, that wasn't news.

I wanted to know why she shot me. He seemed surprised I didn't know. I recalled Chloe said something about Jesus dying for us.

He could only tell me what the media reported. Chloe was in a fringe religious group claiming God was angry with us and He needed a sacrifice. Apparently, I was the sacrifice. Seems when they arrested her Chloe was saying I was so perfect God couldn't bear to make another. Strange commendation.

I lay there piecing together what the surgeon had said with what I knew of Chloe. It jostled into place like ice growing on a lake. All I could think of saying was, it would have been nice of them to ask me first.

He said I might have declined their offer.

Chloe was in custody, but no one knew where she was held. Police were concerned her friends would try and get her out or that some of my fans might exercise rough justice. Either way, I was safe and would probably make a full recovery, though I'd given the surgeon an anxious five minutes under the knife. Loss of blood triggered a cardiac arrest, but they got me going again.

He asked if I'd had any NDEs. Hadn't a clue what he meant. Near Death Experiences, apparently. White lights. God talking to me.

There were none. Nothing between St Paul's and waking up in hospital.

Better that way, he said. Less confusing. I'd feel rough for a few days, but that was to be expected.

The surgeon left me in peace. I lay there thinking of Chloe and hoping she was okay. There was something fragile about her and even if she was insane, and I guessed she must be, that just made her more fragile.

Next day the story was in the press that my first words were to ask if she was okay. It created a bit of a fuss on the ward as they tried to blame someone for breach of confidentiality. I got an apology. That afternoon I dictated a statement for the press and TV. Nothing much, just saying I was okay and I held no grudge. I asked for the crowd outside the hospital to go home as they were blocking the entrances. Most of them did.

Done with the axe. Andreas and I have firewood for the next few days. I'll cut more tomorrow for when I return here: if I return here. No, I'm confused. When I return: I am to bury Andreas someday. Perhaps sooner than I expected; he's been drinking most of today. Leaving him be and finding things to keep me busy. Do I regret my offer? A little, but what else could I have done?

...

That noise is me sharpening the axe. Putting an edge on iron is one of those tasks man has done for two thousand and more years. Later, I'll sit and watch the sun go down. There's smoke from Andreas's cook fire so at least he isn't too drunk to make food.

I'll keep talking. That evening at the hospital I had a visitor. Jack Regis, of all people. Wanted to prove not everyone at GeriCo was a nut-job, as he phrased it. He asked if Stenson had visited me. She hadn't. Maybe tomorrow, Jack said. God you're a mess. Silly bitch nearly did for you. Have some grapes.

He brought me the least imaginative hospital gift of all, but blunt-speaking, uncouth Jack Regis was just the sort of lift I needed.

I said at least Chloe wasn't a decent shot and asked if it was true she'd left GeriCo. He said not exactly. Didn't know the full story, but there one day, gone the next. Security had stopped her entering. Something to do with the Jesus freaks she was with.

Had he known about her crazy friends? He denied it, saying he only knew what was on the media. Then he said I looked a bit like Jesus. I said fuck off. He said I needed a haircut and get rid of the 'tache. I started to laugh and immediately regretted it. Painkillers were only so good. Had to remind Jack I had stitches.

Shame, he said. And him with a wicked sense of humour. Then he surprised me. My old job was waiting for me, if I wanted it. Said they'd have me like a shot, no joke intended.

Asked him why. Said I gave GeriCo respectability, all that last-born business. Look, he said, I know you don't like talking about it, but fuck me, Kit; you're the last fucking human born on this planet. You gave us some dignity. Now we're just trying to make the best of a crap situation. He said what happened at Worcester wouldn't be the last. There'd be more and worse fuck-ups. If not by GeriCo then by others.

I said he was arguing for cheap labour. Opening the border to Africans. He denied it. There was no answer because at some point, there'd be no one left to wipe anyone's arse.

Jack had a plan. It was a private room but discussing suicide demands hushed voices. I kept my voice down.

He'd seen the future, just as I had, but I was blessed because I could buy my way out of it. Said he would punch me, wounded and all, if I offered him charity. I wouldn't do that to him. He said I'd offered to help Chloe and her grandmother. I admitted it. The grandmother had died a few months ago. Maybe that had tipped Chloe over.

I said money was all I had to offer people. Hated to see suffering.

But I wasn't to worry about old Jack. He'd know when it was time. Hop on a boat for a cruise. He asked me if I thought warm or cold was best. Didn't know what he meant. The water, he said. He hated the cold. I said cold would be quicker.

So it's the fjords, he said. Pissed on vodka and ups-a-daisy. He raised a hand on two fingers and mimed walking off the edge of the bed. Then he asked me what I was doing. Said I didn't know, but thought of getting away from everything.

Jack said to keep in touch and not to put a door between me and the world. If he could stand the place so could I. I was still in the prime of life, barely thirty, but should look out for the nutters.

He was right, but I didn't heed him. I did put a door between me and the world and Andreas has kicked it open. I'd better go see what he's doing. The sun's gone down.

Transcript 024

Kit: You don't want to say anything?

Andreas: No. Have a drink.

Kit: I think I've had enough.

Andreas: Gamó. You will not refuse my wine. This is my house.

Kit: You can take this with you.

Andreas: Ai sto diaolo.

Kit: Okay. But I'll regret it.

Andreas: I will make sure you regret it. You want me to be grateful? Well, I am, but do not expect me to be happy.

Kit: Not now. I need some air.

Andreas: Where are you going?

Kit: Out, clear my head.

Andreas: There is nothing there. It is midnight. You will fall and break a leg, then what?

Kit: I need to be alone, sorry.

Andreas: Then go, fool. Wine is my friend.

...

Kit: I'm outside. Christ, it's dark. Waiting for my eyes to get used to it. At least I've a torch. Got the wine glass with me. Don't want to finish it. Had enough. Christ knows what he makes it from. Leaving the glass on a wall.

Not staying here tonight. Can't stand it any longer. Have to tell Andreas. Don't want him waiting up all night thinking I've fallen or got lost. Going back inside. With glass.

Andreas: You saw sense, then?

Kit: No. If you're going to be like this, I'll spend the night on the boat. Bringing back your glass.

Andreas: *Gamó! Vlacas.* Leave me be.

Kit: Get some sleep.

...

Stepping away from the door.

...

That noise was the glass against the inside of the door. I should have left it out here. Chloe's trial will need to wait. I can't talk to you while groping around in the dark. Got the torch, but it's been in my pocket all day. Only one bar of charge left. About twenty minutes. Peering at the ground. What is life if we never take risks? Longer, perhaps. Path's level here. Moonlight should be enough. Turning the torch off to save energy. Path's paler than the surroundings and smoother underfoot. Head's throbbing. Drunk far too much. Excuse me. I must do this.

...

Can't remember when last I made myself ill. Swilling my mouth with water. Going carefully down to the jetty. Need to concentrate. There's the white of the waves on the beach. You can hear them.

…

On the jetty. Don't walk off the damn edge. Need the torch. Top of the ladder. Boat's below. Ladder's cold and my hands are too sore to grip. Climbing down to my boat. Reaching out my foot. Deck's moving a bit. Must be a swell. Or maybe I'm drunk. I am drunk. But it's my space here. Had forgotten how hard company is when you're not used to it. Please, let him not be so angry in the morning. Going below. Got power. Solar panel on the cabin roof has done its job. I'd read, but I want to tell you of the trial. Chloe's trial. The woman who tried to kill me, make me a fucking Christ for the End Times.

Shit, sorry, I'm pissed. It was insane to come down here in the dark. Now I've dropped the fucking torch. There it is. Good. Still works. But maybe no more talking. Not when I'm like this. Tell you in the morning. Listen to this, if I can work the machine. You have it of course, the repository will have the recording, and you won't hear me breathing over it. Here. Listen. Thomas Tallis from five-hundred years ago when the world was young. Listen. Listen, for Christ's sake.

…

Seems I didn't turn you off last night. Recorder's powered by a motion sensor. I move it charges. Surprised I haven't drained its cell. Light's showing so must be okay. Can't erase the recording so you've six hours of me snoring. Spent one quarter of my life asleep and that's what I sound like. Good morning. I must eat something. Biscuits will do for now. Not ready to face Andreas yet. Still early. Sun through the decklight woke me. Hours before I can start raking salt. No excuse, then. On with the story.

Chloe's trial started ten months after she tried to kill me. Her lawyer argued for manslaughter on the grounds of diminished responsibility. I'd have accepted that but prosecution wanted murder. The trial was at the Old Bailey. I was offered police protection. Investigation had found several groups interested in my death. Did I tell you that the night I was born a woman had her baby torn to pieces in India? They thought she'd put a hex on the women in the village stopping them from conceiving. Thirty years on and I'd become the hex, only this was London. I took the offer. Couldn't accept I was in real danger, but I had a scar to prove otherwise. Must have believed Chloe was a one off; a religious freak, like the guy who shot Professor Baxter. Turned out Chloe knew all about him: among her friends he was a hero for stopping Baxter.

Her lawyer's second defence was arguing Chloe was a pawn used by others to get at me. They called themselves *Lazarenes*, after Lazarus in the Bible. Like Lazarus, mankind would rise from the dead, but only once they got rid of me. They'd collected every bit of news about me into a kind of shrine. There was video footage of me at Worcester, as a newborn in my mother's arms, even at my father's funeral. I watched it in the prosecutor's office for over an hour until I couldn't bear it any longer.

Five days a week for a month I commuted to the Old Bailey in the back of an unmarked police car. It was like some kind of strange job where I had to do nothing except look like I was listening, except for the two days I took the witness stand.

Chloe stared in front of her the whole time. I don't think she ever looked at me. Whether she regretted it, or only regretted I was still alive, I never knew. In the evenings and weekends I'd hide away and ignore the phone and email. Despite Jack Regis's advice, I was turning away from the world. But you can't blame me for that. Chloe got indefinite detention in a mental hospital. Reckoned that was the best thing for her, and for everyone else. After the verdict I wanted to creep out the back way and ignore the press but it wasn't an option. So I braved it out. Hated those flashguns. Yes, I bore her no ill. She was clearly unwell. No lasting damage. Full recovery. Nothing more to say. I have nothing more to say.

Then Joan got in touch again. She'd been following it on the news. Did I want to meet? I looked round at my apartment. It was a mess. I remembered the plants overflowing her walls, like the Hanging Gardens of Babylon. I reminded her the last woman to ask me on a date had tried to kill me. She said she'd moved to the country and had met some good people. Wanted me to meet them. Gave me some info to check online so I'd know they were okay. She said I'd looked awful on the TV. I said TV hadn't lied.

She gave me their name and I checked them out. Somerset was as country as I'd ever been in England and I couldn't hide away forever. It was January: start of a new year.

I had better see if Andreas is in a good mood this morning. I suspect not.

Transcript 025

Kit: Bagging salt. Left it in the sun to burn off any damp from the night and it's running, dry as sand, into duralene sacks. I made these myself, cutting and sewing from an old set of sails. The authorities cleared the island of useful supplies when they evacuated everyone so now it's make do and mend. Andreas is suffering this morning. Didn't stop drinking after I left him last night. He's bitter at me for leaving him alone. We're sailing tomorrow first light. Want to anchor at Marathias before dark. Won't take me long to bag all this. Then I'll help Andreas get his things aboard. Told me there's another well by the olive orchard but the winding gear is broken. Want to see if it's repairable. If I'm to live here after Andreas is gone, then I can't rely on a single well.

Where was I on my story? Joan, second time I met Joan. Met her at Bristol train station and she drove me down to Glastonbury. Music festival was long gone but she said you could still buy a witch's cauldron or get your chakras massaged on the High Street. The Brotherhood of the Oak was one of several fringe end-timer groups flourishing in the shadow of paganism. Maybe after Chloe's brush with the Lazarenes I should have been more wary, but Joan was always level-headed. She wouldn't be mixed up in anything crazy. I remember it was a cold, bleak day as we left Bristol.

I asked her what her friends did. Said they sang songs, chanted. Into tree-worship. She got my attention when she said they danced naked around a bonfire.

I asked what they burnt on the fire, if not trees. She said I was still a cynical bastard, which was true, but in my defence I said I'd been shot at. Twice.

Back then, I didn't know the old meaning of *bonfire*. Always assumed it was French, a *good fire*, a cheerful fire. It isn't; it's *bone* fire; a fire of bones.

Joan was different. The weight of expectation she carried around, the weight she partially exorcised by cramming her flat with greenery, that was gone. I liked that.

Joan had met this group through Dignity, a group campaigning for better ways to die. Joan was a member. I asked about her collection of plants. They were gone, all gone.

She accused me of not liking them and I said I wasn't cut out to be Tarzan. You were never king of my jungle, she said.

Her new place was decorated white. Very calming. Very Zen. Everything she was saying suggested she was something of a rarity: a person who was growing more sane and reasonable, not less.

I said something about Kew losing its rival. She laughed and said I must have thought she was crazy and the only reason I'd kept quiet was in case she stopped fucking me. Said she was pretty accurate, but plants weren't people. She needed people. We all need people. I sang an old song, from years before I was born. *Find me somebody to love.*

She said no. No more love. I agreed, we were just friends. I was lying, but I gave that round to Joan. The weekend would be long. She was okay looking, I knew what she was like in bed and she wasn't crazy. We all need goals in life.

…

I've found a barrow. Frame's wobbly and the steel base has split, but it will serve. Wheel is bare steel and rattles over the stony path between the saltpan and the jetty. Axle's squealing like a cat and I've nothing to grease it.

…

Can barely hear myself over the din. You, too, I suppose, can barely hear me. I have, I think, almost my bodyweight in salt and carry the sacks one at a time.

…

Andreas is bringing stuff down to the jetty. His whole life's here. He's on the path, hands clasped under a pile of books, knees apart and back bowed. I'm standing here like Papa stood fifty years ago in front of the family car and wondering how everything would fit in. There's a row of books six metres long.

Stacking the salt at the edge of the jetty, well away from Andreas's things. Have to remind him there's a limit to how much I can take: Hey! My boat doesn't need any more ballast.

Andreas: Ballast! Damn you! This is *learning*.

Kit: Looking at the titles. They're old. Printed decades, a century even, before the Barren. Most are Greek but there's a few German and English titles. Opening the cover of one. Stamped property of Athens University, or that's what I assume the faded purple means. Wind is unfurling the pages. He's using pebbles for paperweights.

Where did you get these?

Andreas: I stole them. So what? They would not get read and loved where they were, so I took them. You have room in that thing? I cannot leave these.

Kit: I hope so, but I can't promise. I came for salt, not books.

Andreas: The whole sea is salt. These are irreplaceable.

Kit: You think I'm a Philistine?

Andreas: Eh?

Kit: You think I don't value things.

Andreas: You have forgotten how to. I have more to bring.

Kit: He's walking back to the house. He's stubborn, give him that. Wish I knew if this is the right thing to do. Can't linger. I need to get on.

Jumped onto the boat. From here I can reach up and grab hold of the sacks. Damn heavy. Duralene is tearing at my hands. Bleeding at the knuckles. Need these packed carefully below. Can't have them shifting when we're underway. I'm weary, though. Back and shoulders are slowly seizing up. Want good weather and a fair sea tomorrow. Andreas is returning with more books. He's staggering under the weight. Damn fool will kill himself. No point interfering. Hope we can get them all on the boat. Be a god-awful scene if we can't. I'm waiting for him to get in earshot.

Andreas, if I am –

Andreas: If you are what? To inherit my island?

Kit: Not exactly what I meant.

It's exactly what I meant, but not in those terms.

Andreas: I cannot be without books. A man builds what life he can. I lose my island, my home, because I am too old to care for them. But deny me a book when I can still read, damn you, you *son of a cunt*. Know how hard this is to do?

Kit: That went well. His glance was sharp as a knife. Now he's off again, returning for Christ knows what. More books? His back is less bent now he has nothing to carry. Except that's an illusion. He's carrying everything.

The wind lifts the cover of a book. I weigh it down with a pebble. Need to get these sacks below. Need my breath.

Ω

Kit: Joan's cottage belonged to a friend. She wanted me to know she'd come into money. It was near a place called Wells and it was freezing. I helped get logs in from the wood store. There was a hill in the distance with some kind of church on it. I asked if it was Glastonbury Tor. It was. That was where Joan's friends lit their fires and danced. I said there weren't any trees and she said they took the trees with them. I had a vision of something out of Macbeth. I wasn't far wrong. They carried it all to the summit. Joan said all this land was forest once and would be again, after we'd gone. They were honouring the return of nature. That was Nature, with a capital 'N'. Mother Nature, the earth goddess.

I asked if they danced naked on the hill around their bonfires. Joan laughed and said I'd get to see her naked, along with a few dozen other naked bodies, one of which would be mine. It was January. Joan said I'd get used to the cold. I'm at least half-Greek. I never get used to the cold. Two day's time, we'd be climbing naked up the hill. I said she could have warned me. She said I'd be naked. Wasn't as if I had to bring anything with me. We'd do it at night. No one would see us.

After Chloe, I should have known better. I'm a slow learner.

Going out for more wood, I stopped a while and stared at the tower on the hill and imagined a load of pale-fleshed bodies flagellating their way up it. For whatever reason, it didn't bother me much. I'd seen crazier things.

Stowing the last sack of salt aboard. Andreas is on the jetty. He's pacing up and down and muttering.

Is this everything you want me to take?

Andreas: There is a chair. Belonged to my father. Cannot carry it alone.

Kit: And then nothing more to come down?

Andreas: This is all. Everything. And the chair.

Kit: Can you bring it here and I'll see to stowing it safely.

Andreas: It will all go?

Kit: I can't promise, but I'll try. Don't want to make a second trip. It's late in the year. I was lucky with the weather this time and there's things I have to do before winter. Just pray we don't hit bad weather. No, promise me that we save ourselves and the boat first. Never liked the idea of drowning.

Andreas: Your boat. And my father's chair?

Kit: Later. This won't take long. Before we leave, I want to look at that well by the olive grove.

Andreas: It is broken.

Kit: It might be repaired. If I *am* one day to look after your house and keep your grave, I can't rely on a single well.

Andreas: You think like a young man. You make plans.

Kit: You do not?

Andreas: Not any more. And turn that thing off. This is too miserable to record.

Kit: Okay. Done.

Transcript 026

Kit: Had to lash the chair on deck, but everything else has gone below. Be a squeeze sleeping aboard tomorrow night. Left the boat now. Walking up towards the olive grove.

It was near sunset when Joan and I entered the wood. Dead leaves crackled underfoot. The evergreen mass of a yew or holly punctuated the winter woodland with midnight.

I told Joan I had no idea what I was supposed to be looking for. She said firewood. We were surrounded by wood.

She waved a branch. Didn't look like it would burn for long and the day was grey and cold. I doubted we'd have warmer weather this evening. I found a sawn log and hefted it onto my shoulder. She thought I was crazy, but I said she'd be glad of it later. At least I'd get warm carrying it up the hill. Got back to Joan's car. Dropped the log inside. She wedged the thick end of her branch between the front seats and the back of it stuck out a rear window. The wood was damp. Joan said I was complaining about the weather. It was January, it's meant to be awful. I meant the wood. The wood was damp. It wouldn't burn.

She said Chris would get it going.

Joan had said a lot about Chris. It was odd hearing his name on Joan's lips, given he and I were almost namesakes. In a spasm of jealousy, I wondered if there was anything between them. Chris was the leader of this merry band. From what Joan told me, there was nothing he didn't have an answer to.

Did he say spells or rub two sticks together? I asked her.

She guessed I didn't like Chris but I said, reasonably, that I wouldn't know if I liked him until I'd met him.

Chris got it to burn with spirits. I assumed she meant petrol, but it was whisky or vodka. Whatever Chris thought was right. It was an offering to nature. Did I have my doubts by then? Oh yes, but only about the sanity of it all and whether I'd freeze to death. But Joan would, or so she said, be stark naked, and I had ideas for warming us up afterwards.

Ha! Climbing a path in full sun, hat protecting my head from the heat, and I'm telling you about a cold January evening. It gets damp here in winter but never seen a frost. The cold has its uses. It kills off pests. That doesn't happen here so much.

Andreas's olives will be ready in a few weeks. It seems criminal to let a good harvest go to waste but there's my own harvest and a roof to repair. Can't be in two places and Andreas ought not to be left alone. At least, not for more than a day and this would take a week. Trees won't hurt to be left for a few seasons. Andreas never pruned them last year. Can tell by the pattern of growth. They'd bear twice as much with better care. But they're not why I'm here. Found the well. The shaft's intact and the stonework looks good. The wooden parts are rotten but I can reuse the steel bearings, axle, pawl, and ratchet. Nothing important is missing. The rope has gone but I've spare. One more thing. Got a stone. Leaning over the shaft and letting go.

Hear that? I've got water. Maybe ten metres down. Hard to tell.

Could return to the boat now. Left Andreas adding a few things to what he's taking. But I can't help him choose and my presence only annoys him. So, I'm climbing again. Up through the abandoned terraces, following the route I took yesterday. I tell myself it's to survey the island, or as much as I can of it, but the real reason is to look across at Kyrios. *Maria Vitalis*: Mary of life. Climbing this reminds me of climbing Glastonbury Tor, though the outcomes are, I hope, very different.

Joan parked on one of the lanes around the back of the town and we walked up between high banks and hedgerows. She had a torch but the light was feeble. I only had a cigarette lighter. We were still clothed at that point. The nakedness came later. Other pinpricks of light followed us on the road and some came down from in front. We converged at a gate below the hill. Others had already gathered on the far side of the gate. Most were naked. I guessed this was it. We got inside the gate and stripped silently. The Greek in me protested, but I remembered my father and dragged the log of wood onto my shoulder and stood there like an idiot. Couldn't see a damn thing.

Others arrived, most carrying lanterns and torches you could actually see with. A lot of us were far older than I expected and some were in wheelchairs. The log was cold and brutally hard. At one point it felt like a load of insects had run out of it and down my chest. Dropped the damn thing, only just missing my foot and did a little war dance, brushing the creatures off me. Joan got her torch on me. It was just a few flakes of wood.

She said I shouldn't have picked something so heavy. Her branch lay over her shoulder; I doubt it was any heavier than a broom. I muttered they'd all be grateful when I got it to the top. I could sense her shrug even in the darkness. Then she nudged me playfully, saying she was naked and that was what I was hoping for.

Not in the pitch fucking dark it wasn't.

Pale flesh glimmered all around in the yellow light. I asked about the wheelchairs. Were they all going to make it? Joan said it's what they wanted.

Chris was the only one wearing anything other than shoes. Looked like a baseball cap, or maybe a Jewish skullcap. He also had a shepherd's crook.

Joan introduced me. I was just Kit, no mention of my mother's name. We waited what must have been another ten minutes while a few stragglers arrived, including an old guy bent over a walking frame. He had pale hair all over his back and ribs showing through his sides. I wondered if this was a pilgrimage for the old and the lame, like Lourdes.

Then we were walking and the crowd became an illuminated daisy chain winding through the darkness.

Enough for now. Andreas is right. I'm spending too long in the past. See half the island now. The rest is hidden behind higher ground to the north of me. Brought my field glasses and I'm searching along the coast for a place where I can lay the boat up for winter. Andreas's jetty is too exposed. Looking at a bay sheltered on three sides which might do. Turning the glasses across the sea toward Kyrios. Pines and rocks. Not as mountainous as this island and it's more wooded. Something is glinting at me, reflecting the sun. It can only be glass. Can't see anything more. A lizard runs near my feet, darting like quicksilver and then standing in the sun. Insects hum. Will this be my home too?

Transcript 027

Kit: You're ready?
Andreas: No.
Kit: We have to go.

Andreas: You have to go.

Kit: We've been through this. If you stay you'll die.

Andreas: I will die anyway. How long have you got? How long?

Kit: Years yet.

Andreas: Why the fuck bother?

Kit: I can't leave you here like this.

Andreas: I know.

Kit: Then are you ready to leave?

Andreas: No, but as you make so plain, I have no choice. You give me no choice.

Kit: If I hadn't come here, if I hadn't lost my salt and had to come here, you'd be dead.

Andreas: I would, yes. And we would not have this talk. That storm of yours was unfortunate for both of us. Lead on. I shall follow.

Kit: Don't keep me waiting. I want to make Marathias before nightfall.

Leaving him be for the moment and walking down to the boat. Hoping he gets a move on. Everything he wants from the house is stripped out and packed aboard. Christ knows, it isn't much to show for an entire life. Perhaps it would have been better had I not showed up here and then at some future date I'd have found his corpse and buried it. He seems to think so.

But I can't leave him now. He argues with everything I say and I haven't had to say so much in years. It's exhausting. The weather is perfect. No sea to speak of and a decent breeze. Time's wasting. Was it always so hard negotiating with people? Dealing with differences of opinion, thoughts, and feelings? It must have been, except now I can't walk away.

I'm on the jetty staring back at his house and waiting for him to appear. This is insane. If he doesn't show I'll spend the day aboard.

May as well carry on. Halfway up Glastonbury Tor and I'm wondering why we're here. No moon. Hardly any light from the town below. Joan and I were near the head of the line a few metres behind Chris who led the way with a massive lantern. Joan pushed an old man in a wheelchair. I helped her get it up the steps. Can't recall the invalid's name. Not certain he ever said it. Mostly he apologised for the fuss.

The group stretched out by the pace of the slowest member. The halt and the Zimmer-framed. Any idea that it would be fun to see Joan naked had vanished. The whole thing was miserable. I'd no idea what the point was, I was cold, and that log was too heavy. Halfway up the old guy stopped apologising and whenever I caught him in the torch beam he looked half-frozen.

I asked Joan what was going on. She said it was a re-birthing. But she didn't mean like born-again Christians.

I've still no idea how high that hill is. I got to the top having stubbed my toes twice and my foot run over by the wheelchair. We sheltered within and around the tower on the summit. Up close it was just a ruin. The wind cut through us and Joan let me hug her. There was this huge sense of space, as though there was nothing around us. Far off there were lights, a town or a city, I couldn't tell. We'd dropped our wood on a pile. Someone, I think it must have been Chris, helped the old guy out of the chair. I hadn't given it a thought, but seemed he could walk, just not very well. I didn't see where Chris took him.

I sat in the wheelchair to give my feet a break. Then some bloke tried to lead me away by the hand. Course, didn't fancy that, but he looked violent. Joan spoke up for me and he disappeared. Still didn't know what was happening. Didn't get it until we started down and the wheelchair was still empty.

I said we couldn't do it. They'd all freeze to death. Joan said I shouldn't make trouble. I didn't understand what she was saying. This was murder. She said it's what they'd wanted. Had any of them protested? I admitted none had. They'd been led away like lambs. Is this why I'm giving Andreas such a hard time? I'm not letting the old bastard lie down like they did.

I wish Joan had told me what it was really about.

Some in the group overheard us arguing. Chris stepped closer. Asked Joan if anything was wrong. She said no. I said yes. This was all wrong.

He said it would be quick and the "energies" whatever that meant, made this a good place to pass over. People had been coming to this place for thousands of years.

Didn't believe him. He didn't care, but said it was better if I never returned. I agreed.

Joan wasn't impressed with me. I asked if she had a thing for Chris and she accused me of jealousy. Fair point. Accused me of killing people in GeriCo's factories. Said at least they weren't murdered. She said it was a living death and gave me the wheelchair to push, thinking it might keep me busy and quieter. There was no pushing needed, but it was hard to steer on the slope. Behind us, the top of the hill had vanished against the night sky.

Someone had –

Andreas: Hey! You on the boat?

Kit: I'm below. Wait.

Andreas: So there you are. Thought you had sailed away.

Kit: You'd rather I had?

Andreas: I would not have objected.

Kit: Don't believe you. Wait. I'll help you on. I assume you're coming.

Andreas: Easier for me to go than stay. Everything of mine is on this thing. I am the only part missing.

Kit: It's for –

Andreas: Do not tell me it's for the best. I will not like your robot. Never have liked them.

Kit: I know. I've got a parrot.

Andreas: Stupid creatures. This thing safe?

Kit: Thought you wanted to die?

Andreas: I do not want to drown. I want a grave. I want that woman to come here and weep over my grave. You will do that?

Kit: I promise.

Andreas: That thing. I see a red light.

Kit: It's recording, yes.

Andreas: No one will want to hear this. And no one will.

Kit: Maybe not. I was talking to it about Joan.

Andreas: The mad woman?

Kit: Yes. And I realised why I'm so fucking determined not to leave you to die here.

Andreas: You have? I admit I wondered.

Kit: Get on and I'll tell you.

Andreas: I will, but turn that thing off first.

Kit: Why?

Andreas: I don't want it to hear an old man cry.

Transcript 028

Kit: You're okay with it now?
Andreas: Now? Yes.
Kit: You didn't want it to record when we left.

Andreas: I did not.

Kit: The boat feels different with another person on board.

Andreas: You say I weigh too much?

Kit: No. Far from it. You need to put on weight.

Andreas: Well then?

Kit: Just different. I'm aware of another person aboard. I'm so used to being on my own.

Andreas: I never got used to it. Who got closest to being your wife? That mad woman?

Kit: Joan? Maybe. At least she didn't shoot me.

Andreas: What happened to her?

Kit: She fell in with a weird crowd. I kept away. Once I knew what they were doing.

Andreas: What were they doing?

Kit: Killing people.

Andreas: Murder?

Kit: Mercy killing, they called it.

Andreas: Drugs?

Kit: They let them freeze to death.

Andreas: Ach. That's not so bad.

Kit: You weren't there.

Andreas: You were not in Athens. That was hell. I watched my wife die so do not talk to me of good and bad ways to die. Hers was the worst.

Kit: I'm sorry.

Andreas: Why?

Kit: Because I forgot. I know what happened.

Andreas: You know only what I told you. I could tell that machine of yours.

Kit: I thought you hated it.

Andreas: I do. But if anyone ever listens to this thing they will get bored of you, you, you all the time.

Kit: Meant to be my story.

Andreas: And I am part of your story. I am here, now. As are you. Give the thing to me and I'll say something.

Kit: No.

Andreas: Why not?

Kit: You might chuck it overboard. Wouldn't put it past you. Stay there and talk. Speak clearly.

Andreas: No interrupting me. Agree to that?

Kit: Agreed. I can think about sailing.

Andreas: Boat sails itself.

Kit: I wish. Tell it your name first.

Andreas: I know what to say. I'm no fool. My name is Andreas Alexandris and unlike your fool owner I am full Greek, born in Athens. My father also. My mother came from a village. She never liked the city. I had three older brothers and one sister who was younger. She was my mother's last child. You know what happened after that. Greece was full of old people. Nothing has changed. Nothing more to say.

Kit: Short and sweet, as they say.

Andreas: Not so sweet. How do you find so much to talk about?

Kit: Arrogance, I suppose. My story's unique. Stuff happened that I remember; stuff that could only have happened to me.

Andreas: Lots of people got shot. Died years before they should have done.

Kit: I know. I was shot by someone who thought God was angry with everyone. That was unusual.

Andreas: Madness is more common than you think.

Kit: Maybe.

Andreas: That woman. The one you almost married. What happened to her? No, tell me; did she murder a lot of people?

Kit: I don't think she murdered anyone.

Andreas: She let them freeze to death, sounds like murder to me.

Kit: Shit.

Andreas: What did I say?

Kit: I liked her, Andreas. That's all. The worst of it, they didn't all freeze to death.

Andreas: Who?

Kit: The old people.

Andreas: What happened then?

Kit: They wheeled them up to the top of a hill.

Andreas: Tall as the hill on my island?

Kit: Maybe. But it was cold, cold as it gets here in the winter. We were all naked. Me, Joan, the old people. Everyone. We left them at the top of the hill in the middle of the night so they'd freeze to death. But not all of them stayed there. I think some changed their mind. Only that wasn't part of the deal. I think they were just murdered.

Andreas: You think?

Kit: It was dark. I couldn't tell. Some people, some of those with Joan, they had clubs. Weapons. I heard things.

Andreas: But she didn't do anything.

Kit: She was part of it.

Andreas: What is that English phrase. Guilt by…

Kit: Guilty by association. You're guilty for the crime of your friend because you were there.

Andreas: So, you are a hypocrite also.

Kit: Why? I didn't know they were going to do that.

Andreas: Not you and that mad woman. Who you worked for, Gerry-whatever it was. You killed thousands. Maybe millions.

Kit: People die. We had to do something. Nobody froze to death: not through intention. There were mistakes, but it wasn't murder.

Andreas: You believe that?

Kit: I...

Andreas: What are you doing?

Kit: Turning this off.

Andreas: So it does not hear my screams as you drown me?

Kit: No. I just want to think.

Andreas: Ah. Bad idea. Drinking, yes. But no thinking.

Ω

Andreas: Is it on?

Kit: Yes.

Andreas: So, this is your island. I do not think so much of it.

Kit: I don't live in Marathias. I don't think it's safe.

Andreas: Ghosts?

Kit: No ghost. Wild dogs. But everything's been stripped out. Nothing to eat here. My stores are at home.

Andreas: I knew this place when it was still a town with people.

Kit: So did I.

Andreas: It will be cosy on this little boat tonight. I think I snore. And I know I fart. Age. Can't help it.

Kit: I'll sleep on deck. You're right, it's cramped below...

Andreas: What is wrong?

Kit: Nothing. Only a dog came on board when I was here last.

Andreas: Should we keep watch, like real sailors?

Kit: For one dog? No, I've a better idea. We go ashore. If we see a dog we make friends with it.

Andreas: Or shoot it and be done with it.

Kit: I'll take the gun. But I don't think it's dangerous.

Andreas: Dead dog is not dangerous.

Kit: I'd sooner not.

Andreas: He kills a million poor bastards and spares one dog.

Kit: You want me to wish I'd never found you, keep talking.

Andreas: I was waiting for you to guess. Like you. I have had no one to talk to in a long, long time.

Kit: What about the woman you mentioned.

Andreas: She rarely calls.

Kit: I'm not surprised. Can you get up onto that trawler? Its deck is sound. Easiest way ashore. We'd better do it while there's still some light so we can get firewood.

Andreas: You still recording?

Kit: Yes.

Andreas: Even this? This is no way to treat your audience. Listen, whoever you are. Zachariades saved my fucking life and I know I should be grateful but I am not so sure if I am. Maybe when I die I'll wonder what the fuck I was waiting for. Yes, I can climb up to that boat and I can do what you ask. Firewood, yes. We build a fire and sit all night waiting for a dog that we may, or may not, have to shoot... we could eat the dog: we did in Athens when it got bad.

Kit: I don't want to eat dog. We've dried fish. I can boil it if we have a fire.

Andreas: Then we should not delay.

Kit: As I was saying.

Andreas: Then help me up. I am not a damn monkey and I have ten years on you.

Kit: Only ten?

Andreas: Do not mock your elders.

Kit: I wasn't. I'd just forgotten.

Andreas: Ten years till you are like me. Yes. Don't forget.

Kit: Here.

Andreas: What?

Kit: Step into my hands. I'll help you up. Grab hold of the boat's railing. It's still sound.

Andreas: Rusted to bits.

Kit: It'll hold you.

Andreas: This will not be so dignified.

Kit: I'll turn this off, then.

Andreas: Good. When I die I hope you'll say good things about me into that machine.

Kit: While you're living you can say good words, if you like.

Andreas: I am too old to change my habits. That thing off?

Kit: It is now.

Ω

Kit: It's dark. We've lit a fire in the market square. No sign of the dog.

Andreas: What are you telling it that for?

Kit: Just saying where we are.

Andreas: Say something interesting then. We are in New York. That sound is fireworks not a wood fire and we are surrounded by a thousand people. Okay, so they are very quiet people, but here nonetheless. Go on, make it up. Why not?

Kit: I'm not supposed to.

Andreas: Who will complain? My story is better than yours. Two old men waiting for a dog: where is the joy in that?

Kit: Might be two dogs.

Andreas: Halleluiah.

Transcript 029

Kit: Home, sweet home.

Andreas: So this is it?

Kit: What did you expect? A palace?

Andreas: I do not know. Something… more. Where is this robot? Why is it not here to greet you?

Kit: Probably sleeping.

Andreas: Sleep? Ah, a joke.

Kit: Sort of. It shuts down when it's not needed. Conserves energy.

Andreas: Smart robot. Sleep is good.

Kit: If you help me tie the boat up, I'll introduce you.

Andreas: I do not like robots.

Kit: There's a parrot. A real parrot.

Andreas: Does it speak?

Kit: It swears a lot.

Andreas: Think I will like the parrot. Better having your place near the water's edge. Mine is too far.

Kit: Thank you

Andreas: It was not praise. Just observation. My old legs do not want to walk so much. That recorder on?

Kit: Yes. For the moment.

Andreas: I will say this once. I would be dead if you had not come. I am not so sure that is a good thing. But I would not have seen this.

Kit: You're welcome.

Andreas: So, where is this parrot?

Kit: The boat first.

Andreas: Ach. I am no good tying ropes. See my hands?

Kit: Yes. But you can hold a rope?

Andreas: Ay, ay. I can do so much. You want me to work for my keep?

Kit: It seems fair. What's wrong?

Andreas: Turn that thing off.

Kit: I'm recording. This seemed propitious.

Andreas: Seems what? You with your long words.

Kit: This is Billybones. Say hello, Billybones.

Andreas: Why he not speak?

Kit: Guess he's not used to other people.

Andreas: Stupid bird.

Billybones: Stooo-pid.

Andreas: Ha! So it talks. Say something more, stupid bird.

Kit: That's maybe not the way.

Andreas: What is?

Kit: It's nervous of you.

Andreas: Why is it nervous of me? Stupid bird. So this robot. This I must see.

Kit: He likes to sit under that tree.

Andreas: Likes?

Kit: I guess. He goes there.

Andreas: He?

Kit: Sometimes I call it a he. Sometimes not. I have my ways, Andreas. Guess I'm stuck with them. Too much time on my own.

Andreas: Me the same. See robot, yes?

Kit: Go on then. I need to do things inside. Don't wander too far.

Andreas: Ay, ay, ay.

Kit: Andreas is going to find Wendy. I'm going inside, mostly to get away from Andreas. Haven't felt so interrogated since Mama was alive. Need to get the salt off the boat and in the store. Boat's always damp and the salt will suck it up. Don't know whether I can get finished in daylight. Switching this off. I'll tell Andreas to make himself at home. Think I can trust him. Deep down he's grateful. He likes complaining and

I give him someone to complain to. Wendy won't do anything foolish even if Andreas orders him to walk off a cliff. Would it annoy him if I said there are two Wendies –one still crated up and not used? Maybe. Keep that to myself. Everything wears out; joints fail, electrical contacts erode, and there are no user-serviceable parts on a Wendy.

$$\Omega$$

…

Kit: Say again.

Andreas: I said you're nearly done.

Kit: Nearly. Wanted to get finished before nightfall. But…

Andreas: You could have asked.

Kit: Yeah. Maybe I should have.

Andreas: Heavy?

Kit: Ten kilos each. More or less. Much as I want to carry anyway. Be careful with it.

Andreas: Ah. You cannot say I did not try. My back does not like me anymore. Once, give me work and I would do it willingly. Now not so much.

Kit: Understand. I'll get these up to the store and leave the rest for tonight. Think you can get me something to eat?

Andreas: I can try.

Kit: Thanks. I'd like that. If you need anything, ask Wendy. He knows where everything's kept.

Andreas: It will be edible. More I cannot promise.

Kit: Edible is fine.

Andreas is going back to the house. I'm starving, so anything will do. Last few sacks for tonight. My back's sore and my hands are desperate. Can't give this work to Wendy; salt's too corrosive. Had enough of it. Had enough. Hear that? Andreas is whistling to himself in the house. Now he's shouting at Wendy. Picking up a sack. This and two more and I'm finished for the night. Two thirds of the salt is off the boat. Need to check the repair to my store is still good, but that will wait until morning. Stars are out but it's not yet completely dark. Light in the west. I'm dog-weary, as Papa would have said. The sail from Marathias was easy enough, following wind the whole way, but the boat was sitting low in the water so I was anxious the whole time. Now, lifting and carrying exhausts me. Don't expect Andreas to do much. He's got ten years on me, and a harder life has aged him. But it would be good to share labours, as much as I can. As much as he can. Wendy has his uses, but a robot's never companionable. Neither is Andreas, but at least he's no robot.

Tomorrow – yes, making plans, as Andreas said – shift the rest of the salt into the store, then get my roof fixed. Been lucky so far with only that one day of rain, but I have to get it done before autumn. Anxious about climbing the ladder. Andreas can help me with that.

Andreas: What can I do? I hear you out here and I ask myself why is he talking to that machine when he could be talking to me?

Kit: I was saying what I've done today, and what I need to do tomorrow. There's a hole in the house roof needs fixing. Hoping you can help me. Last time I near fell off the ladder. See that tree? Branch came off in a storm and smashed some of the shingles.

Andreas: So, you reckon I can shimmy up there with you? My days as a performing monkey are long-gone.

Kit: No. You can hold the ladder for me. Warn me if I do anything stupid.

Andreas: That is more like it. Cannot let you kill yourself, for who would bury me?

Kit: Good. And there are olives to get in. Nets need repairing.

Andreas: Do that also. The olive is part of my heritage. Greeks and olives go together. When I was young and new-married, I would go with Elena to help her family with the picking. I told you Elena was from a village?

Kit: You did.

Andreas: Poor people, but true Greeks. I got us something to eat. That robot helped. But it was mostly me. You should come in. But turn that off first.

Transcript 030

Kit: That was good.

Andreas: I saw what you did. That little red light is on.

Kit: So it would hear me thank you. Long time since anyone prepared a meal for me.

Andreas: The robot doesn't?

Kit: It's not one of the things he's good at.

Andreas: The rabbit was too salty. You don't need to use so much to preserve it.

Kit: I'd soak it normally, leach the salt out.

Andreas: The water's good here?

Kit: Deep shaft. And I filter it. It's safe.

Andreas: I begrudge you your money, but you spent wisely, I think.

Kit: Thank you. You know I don't have money anymore.

Andreas: You spent it all, all those millions?

Kit: No. But what's left is worthless. Nothing left to buy. What I have here is all I have.

Andreas: Then you are more careful than I am.

Kit: How so?

Andreas: You have more to lose.

Kit: Maybe so. Give me your plate. I'll clean these.

Andreas: So, tomorrow we fix this roof of yours?

Kit: After I've brought up the last of the salt. I also need to wash the boat down.

Andreas: You wash the boat?

Kit: Salt spray, plus the salt in those bags. It's all corrosive. I need to look after it.

Andreas: So many things to care for.

Kit: But you can help me with the roof.

Andreas: And the day after, and the day after?

Kit: Olives.

Andreas: And after the olives?

Kit: What are you saying?

Andreas: You have no books! What do you do with all your time?

Kit: I keep busy. Never been one for reading.

Andreas: So much work just to survive. You have too many things. They suck the time from you. You work to stand still.

Kit: That sounds like Marx.

Andreas: Every Greek was a Marxist. Or a fascist.

Kit: I want to be comfortable. It takes work. After the olives, it's gathering firewood for winter. Wendy can do most of that. Then pruning the olives. That I have to do.

Andreas: You're a martyr to work. Must be the English in you. Come, those are clean enough. We will not die of a speck of grease. What did you do after the woman who killed old people?

Kit: You're interested?

Andreas: I may be the only one who'll ever hear this story. For certain, I am the only human. And you are the only one here to talk to.

Kit: Wait a moment. I'll get a bottle.

Andreas: You have wine?

Kit: I have good wine. This evening deserves good wine. And it will drown the taste of salt.

Andreas: So.

Kit: Drink it slowly. It was expensive.

Andreas: I drink wine. Not money.

Kit: This is forty years old.

Andreas: It's good they made things to last.

Kit: Maybe they didn't think it was over. Maybe this was hope in a bottle.

Andreas: You mean they didn't think it would be us drinking it; two old men staring at the abyss.

Kit: We're not at its edge yet.

Andreas: But we can see it. So, what happened to you after the woman who killed old people? Did anything happen to her?

Kit: I don't know. I never saw her again.

Andreas: Too bad, and you wanted to fuck her.

Kit: I don't know what I wanted. Normality, I suppose. But what was normal? Normal had been thrown out and we made it up as we went along.

Andreas: Still, you wanted to fuck her.

Kit: I wanted to fuck her, yes.

Andreas: So what happened?

Kit: I told you. I never saw her again.

Andreas: But did you hear anything?

Kit: They stopped killing people. Something happened. An investigation. I think the guy who organised it was arrested. Don't know anything else. Or can't recall it.

Andreas: But you, you know what happened to you.

Kit: I went back to writing poetry.

Andreas: Were you any good?

Kit: No.

Andreas: Because you do not read.

Kit: Maybe. Didn't stay at it long but I met someone through poetry. Much better than I was. He was a Buddhist. One way and another, I became a Buddhist and bought my way into a sect in Scotland, on an island. In a monastery.

Andreas: You were a monk? But you don't believe in anything.

Kit: Buddhism didn't have a problem with that. Besides, I believed in me. Started with a month-long retreat. They didn't care who I was, or what I was. They looked after each other.

Andreas: And you were what?

Kit: What do you mean?

Andreas: How old were you?

Kit: Thirty. Maybe thirty-one.

Andreas: So young still. This will be a long story.

Kit: It doesn't seem so.

Andreas: You're fortunate. My youth is like water. I reach out and it falls through my fingers. So, where was this so-called monastery?

Kit: Island, far north of Scotland. Monastery was a converted church. There was a boat to the mainland once a week. Sailed there on a calm evening with the sea almost flat. Felt providential, as though I'd been blessed. It was going to make sense of everything, my father's cancer, of GeriCo, of the Worcester Disaster, of Chloe, and Joan and above all, me. Why me? Why the Barren? Everything. I wasn't looking for God, never have. But I wanted things to make sense.

Andreas: Ah.

Kit: What does that mean?

Andreas: There was your mistake.

Kit: Maybe.

Andreas: Do you want me to say something?

Kit: Can I stop you?

Andreas: You could ask. This is your story.

Kit: No. Speak up. You make me think.

Andreas: That's too bad.

Kit: I'll remember more if you talk.

Andreas: Good. Then I have a purpose. I will be your confessor.

Kit: There's not much sinning from here on.

Andreas: Oh, a shame.

Kit: I'd stay on the island for a month, that's what I told myself. Paid for my lodgings. If it didn't work out, all I'd lost was a bit of cash.

Andreas: All, he says. Many would have changed places with you in an instant and yet your whole life has been a burden to you.

Kit: I don't have anything to compare.

Andreas: Yes you do. If you had any empathy, you would know how fortunate you were.

Kit: There was a girl born just before me. Vietnamese, I think. It was a stillbirth. A bit of luck for her, a bit less for me, and I wouldn't have had this.

Andreas: You'd have exchanged places with that child?

Kit: Maybe. Sometimes thought it would have been better not to see any of this. We all grow old and get used to the idea of dying, but there was always something to pass on. The buds on the trees in winter.

Andreas: Talk about the monastery. I don't like it when you're miserable.

Kit: First night I didn't know what hit me. Whether it was the quiet, or the darkness, I don't know. I cried myself to sleep.

Andreas: Did anyone hear you?

Kit: Hear what?

Andreas: You crying? You slept in what do they call it, with other men?

Kit: A dormitory. No, I had my own room. We all did.

Andreas: That's not a real monastery. No robes? No silence?

Kit: There was silence. At times, anyway. But no robes. It wasn't about suffering for belief. We wanted to find belief in something.

Andreas: But you didn't find it. Am I right?

Kit: It was a respite from all that had happened.

Andreas: You wanted to be a hermit, like you became here.

Kit: I guess.

Andreas: What did they make of you, those not monks?

Kit: The first morning we walked round the island. I think it was to show us the whole of our world. There was no boat on the island. If anyone needed to get off, for an emergency, they'd radio the mainland. We walked for an hour and we're back where we started. Then we ate breakfast. No talking at breakfast. No talking for the whole of the first day.

Andreas: And this is Buddhism?

Kit: Don't know what it was. Some of it was based on Buddhist practice; a lot of it was inspired or created for the moment.

Andreas: You mean like fiction. Made up?

Kit: New times needed new beliefs. Nothing made sense of what was happening.

Andreas: That is true.

Kit: After breakfast they had us digging, except the soil was so thin our spades kept striking rock. Digging in seaweed brought up from the beach. That's how they once farmed on the island. We would have planted potatoes and barley, but it was summer and too late for planting. We did it for the good of working. Work would allow us to be, they said.

Andreas: Who ate the potatoes?

Kit: I did, eventually. We all did. Those who stayed.

Andreas: How long did you stay?

Kit: Two years.

Andreas: More fool you.

Kit: Maybe. If you don't mind, I'll turn this off for now. It's late and I'm tired.

Andreas: We have this wine to drink. I warn you, I snore.

Ω

Kit: I'm weary in limb but my head's restless. Don't know or care what the hour is. Moon's risen and I'm sitting outside. Andreas does snore. Not loudly, but I'm used to silence at night and it disturbs me. I've woken Wendy. Need to ask something.

Kit: Has Andreas asked you to do anything wrong or unusual?

Wendy: Do not comprehend.

Kit: Has Andreas given you an order you could not carry out or did not understand?

Wendy: He uses figures of speech: that is, non-literal statements or questions that are not meaningful or actionable.

Kit: Wendy is nothing if not literal.

Wendy: Do not comprehend. Apologies.

Kit: No matter. I'm recording us. What figures of speech has Andreas directed at you?

Wendy: He said I should boil my head. I did not comprehend meaning. He also said I should take a running jump, but I am not engineered to jump.

Kit: Is that all?

Wendy: It is all Andreas said that I understood. His speech is not always intelligible. He is to stay here?

Kit: For the time being, yes. Why do you ask?

Wendy: Wendy must work for two now. There will be more to do. Request permission to begin scheduled diagnostic on balance sensors and other applications.

Kit: You go then. And yes, you work for two now, but you take orders from me first.

Wendy: Will comply.

…

Wendy's shut down. Can see him standing under his favourite tree. If I lie here much longer, I, too, will fall asleep and then I'll wake up freezing and stiff. Must go in and try to sleep. Need to think straight tomorrow. Goodnight, whoever and wherever you are.

Transcript 031

Kit: I'm turning this on.

Andreas: You're going to talk to yourself? Up there? You're crazy. If you fall I cannot catch you.

Kit: Helps me concentrate. I hope. Want to haul up that bucket, the one with the shingles and the stringer. Steady it for me. Hold the end of the rope.

Andreas: I have it.

Kit: Don't know if I feel better or worse with him here. Not much he can do if I break my neck, and I came close to it last time. Taken as much slack out of the ropes holding the ladder as I can. Shouldn't swing so far over if I lose my balance. The stringer is the right length. I get one end down on the rafter, and then the other. It's at an angle but it doesn't matter. So long as I've something to nail the shingles to.

Wrapping my arms around the ladder. Nails in my left hand, hammer in the right. Wedging the first shingle in place. Tap, tap, get the nail to bite. Now hit it.

First one.

Hoping I don't bend a nail. The metal won't take much more straightening before it snaps. That noise is the shackle rattling against the ladder. Getting my balance right. Next shingle in place. Working up. Overlapping.

Andreas: You're leaning too far over.

Kit: Can't be helped. Not going to reposition the ladder just for this. Too much work. All these ropes to fix. And all for a half-metre. I can do this.

Andreas: Your head, not mine.

Kit: Shit. Andreas, I dropped a nail. If you see it, pick it up.

Andreas: One nail. It's so small.

Kit: Forgot he can't see well. Try again. Shoving the nail into the cedar wood as hard as I can with my thumbnail. Got it. Now, slide it alongside and gently with the hammer. Done. This is working. This feels okay. Next. Can't reach. Okay. Put the nail in the shingle first, then I just have to hold the shingle in place and not worry about the nail dropping. Good. Could have done that on the ground. No matter. Got it in position, and striking home.

Looks like I'm winning this time.

Andreas: You have a care. If you fall you will land on me.

Kit: That's comforting.

Next one. Starting the row above. Sliding it under the row of shingles. It will be watertight, that's all that matters. Hammer. Andreas is peering up at me and shading his eyes against the sky. There's a cool breeze today. Next shingle. Get the nail in it.

Damn. Look out!

Andreas: For what? No, I see it.

Kit: Shingle split when I put the nail in it.

Got another one. That's better. Wood was brittle. Sun does that. In position. And hammer. One more. One more and it's done.

This is the last one. Shingle. Nail. Tap. Tap. Damn, having to reach a long way over. Don't like this. Andreas?

Andreas: I am here.

Kit: See the rope going to that tree?

Andreas: Yes.

Kit: Need you to put your weight on it. Hang on it so I can lean across safely. It'll stop the ladder sliding.

Andreas: If you're sure.

Kit: I'm sure. Just don't jerk it.

Andreas: You want me to hang on it, like a gibbon?

Kit: If you can.

Andreas: I can try.

Kit: Think this will work. His weight will keep the rope in tension. He's doing it. Stay like that until I say. If you've a problem, shout.

Andreas: Don't keep me doing this long.

Kit: I won't.

Now. Shingle. Nail. Leaning over. In position. Having to use the hammer left-handed. This will be fun. Good. Again. Done. Now get yourself together.

Andreas, you can let go.

Andreas: Did it work?

Kit: It worked. It's fixed. Can you take the bucket off me when I lower it?

Andreas: I can. Wait till I am in place. Don't move so fast.

Kit: I'll wait. This is teamwork, you know.

Andreas: Am I better than that robot?

Kit: Much better.

Andreas: That is good.

Kit: Repair's not as pretty as it could be, but it will keep out the weather for another winter. My roof no longer leaks.

I'm lowering it down. Take it from me.

Andreas: I am ready.

Kit: He's waiting, arms outstretched. Almost looks Biblical. Embracing Heaven. If I prayed, I'd offer a prayer of thanks right now.

Andreas: I have it. Are you coming down?

Kit: Hold the ladder for me.

Andreas: I have it. You're a brave man. I could not have climbed up there.

Kit: Brave or stupid. But it's done. I'm not shaking, but I'm glad it's done. Get down on the ground.

Andreas: It's good?

Kit: Good enough. That's all that matters. Thanks.

Andreas: Why you thank me. I did nothing to help.

Kit: It was easier for you being here.

Andreas: Shame you do not have a machine can climb over your roof and fix things.

Kit: If I had found one, I would have bought it, believe me. Ah. There's the nail I dropped.

Andreas: So it is. I meant to tell you it was there.

Kit: Think I'll switch this off now. Let's pack up these things and take a break.

$$\Omega$$

Andreas: Is that thing on again?

Kit: Yes. Just now. Why?

Andreas: Two years, did you say?

Kit: What?

Andreas: With the monks, whatever they believed in. Did anyone fuck anyone on this island?

Kit: Yes. Yes they did. I did.

Andreas: A love affair?

Kit: Sort of.

Andreas: Your love affairs were like plane wrecks. You were happy to walk away from them.

Kit: This was different. She drowned.

Andreas: I'm sorry to hear that.

Kit: Her name was Aileen. She arrived on the island a year after me.

Andreas: So who was on this island? In the beginning?

Kit: About twenty of us. The oldest was around eighty, most in their fifties. More women than men.

Andreas: It was hardest on women. Not having children. In Greece especially.

Kit: I thought so too. Those were the guests, the novices, as they called us. Then there were about a dozen who lived there permanently. The leader was a Frenchman, Joseph Brel.

Andreas: French? Why did a Frenchman go to this place in the middle of nowhere?

Kit: That I never learned. But it was the middle of nowhere. The boat took an hour and then it was thirty kilometres of single-track road back to the nearest big town. In winter it could be hell.

Andreas: Two years! You must have been crazy.

Kit: You think? I was happy there, mostly. Until the last few months. It had been a while since I could say I was happy. I began writing seriously. I kept a journal; we were all encouraged to keep a journal. If this recording I'm making has anything worth saying, it's because of what I did on that island. I learned how to make sense of the world and put it down in words. And no one cared who I was. I liked that. But the winters were hard.

Andreas: Hard enough here.

Kit: Far worse than here. You wouldn't believe it unless you'd seen it. Once a week we had to meet with Brel and tell him what we'd learned about ourselves or had noticed in others or in the world about us.

Andreas: Surveillance?

Kit: But not sinister, I think. It was just to find out about us, and about the health of the community. Any disagreements could be talked out before people got bitter. It was at one of those meetings I learned that Aileen liked me.

Andreas: You had to be told a woman liked you. Had you gone blind?

Kit: A little. I'd grown wary of attachment. I don't think you can blame me for that.

Andreas: Perhaps not. But sure that mad bitch didn't shoot you in the balls?

Kit: Don't talk about her like that.

Andreas: Why not? She tried to kill you?

Kit: Chloe was insane. She didn't know what she was doing and others used her.

Andreas: If you say so.

Kit: That's what the court said.

Andreas: And what does the law know?

Kit: And no, not in the balls. I just kept people at a distance. Especially women.

Andreas: Then what was different about this one?

Kit: I guess we'd both come to the same place. We wanted to make sense of our lives. I didn't want a third winter on my own.

Andreas: Ah, now you're talking sense. A cold bed is no fun.

Kit: True. We have work to do this afternoon. Olive nets need repairing. How are you at sewing?

Andreas: With these hands?

Kit: I know they're bad, but this isn't difficult.

Andreas: I know what it is. I told you, my Elena's family harvested olives. I have mended more nets than you. You have them here?

Kit: No, at Servos. Five kilometres into the hills.

Andreas: Then we should be going.

Kit: I didn't think you would be so keen.

Andreas: Why not? We cannot sit here all the time.

Transcript 032

Andreas: Five kilometres, you say?

Kit: Yes. You've everything you need?

Andreas: I think so. You have water there?

Kit: Never known the well to fail.

Andreas: Then I have everything.

Kit: You'll be okay with the distance?

Andreas: I cannot race along like a child, but I can manage.

Kit: I won't.

Andreas: Then lead on.

$$\Omega$$

Kit: The shade is welcome. The path is almost invisible but I don't lose my place.

Andreas is a few yards behind. I've set an easy pace but don't want him to think it's for his benefit. We've twine and needles for mending the olive nets. Water for the journey, and dried rabbit meat. We'll need something to eat later. The oil will mostly be for fuel. Harvesting will last a week. Optimistically, I'm taking a rifle. There are wild goats near the olive grove and fresh meat makes a change.

Andreas: You are talking to yourself. Muttering into that thing again. I cannot hear a word of it.

Kit: It wasn't for your ears.

Andreas: I know you talk to that thing about me.

Kit: I talk to it about everything.

Andreas: This man you spoke of. The leader?

Kit: You mean Brel?

Andreas: Yes, him. Tell me, if you can, why some men lead and others follow? I have always asked myself that.

Kit: He was inspiring. He inspired me, for a while.

Andreas: He did?

Kit: Yes. When he spoke, you believed him. I believed him. He made the world make sense.

Andreas: So he lied.

Kit: No. What he said was true. Just not the whole truth.

Andreas: And what did he say?

Kit: The old ways of living were no use any more. Everything had changed, so we must change.

Andreas: You went to some hell-cold place to learn that?

Kit: I went there to try and discover how I was to live in a world where nothing made sense any more.

Andreas: Ah. Of course, for ordinary people, people like me, we lived as the world forced us to live. We did what we could to survive and we cared for those we loved. Most of us failed. You could say we all failed. But you, you could play with your life and find whatever meaning you wanted.

Kit: Then why ask me about it if you're just going to be resentful?

Andreas: Resentful? I resent nothing about your life. I had my Elena. I loved her and she loved me. You had nothing in comparison, for all your fame and money. You should envy me.

Kit: Well I don't. I don't envy you.

Andreas: What are you doing?

Kit: Turning this off.

Andreas: You do not want it to hear the truth about your life?

Kit: I want to be quiet and just walk.

Andreas: Then walk.

Ω

Kit: Three days, I think.

Andreas: Three or four, and then only if the weather is good to us. Longer if not.

Kit: You're a pessimist.

Andreas: If you say so, boss.

Kit: The nets are in here.

Andreas: This roof is not so good.

Kit: I know. Big job to repair it. Not worth the time.

Andreas: The time you have left?

Kit: Something like that. Here, help me lay these out. Spread them in the yard outside.

Andreas: Ai! You were not wrong about them. We will be busy.

Kit: Here, needle and thread. Just tie the thread on to what's left. Don't try threading the needle.

Andreas: I could not if I tried.

Kit: How bad are your eyes?

Andreas: Bad enough. But I have seen all I need to.

Kit: How do you read all your books?

Andreas: I remember them, mostly.

Kit: Oh.

Andreas: You wonder why I brought them.

Kit: A bit.

Andreas: Without the book I cannot remember.

Kit: Okay. I'm going to take this net and sit under a tree in the shade. If you need water, the well is over there.

Andreas: When I harvested olives with my wife's family we would have music. Or we would sing as we worked.

Kit: I don't know any of the old songs.

Andreas: And I no longer wish to sing them. Too many memories. How can you live in the past so?

Kit: Do I?

Andreas: All the time, speaking into that machine of yours. First this, and then this. Your whole life spread out like these nets.

Kit: But that's good, isn't it? Reminding ourselves who we are, what we've done. Maybe even understanding why we're here.

Andreas: You sound like you have found God.

Kit: No. Not that. It's as though I've something to say, and I must say it. I was the last man to be born, anywhere and forever. Most of my life I hated being that man, but I can't avoid it now. It shaped my life.

Andreas: Money shaped your life. The rest was fortune, good and ill. Someone had to be last.

Kit: Then that someone would have the same tale as I have, and the same need to tell it.

Andreas: True. And as we have no song, tell your poor tale. This woman on the island, the one who drowned. She was sane?

Kit: Completely sane. Her name was Aileen.

Andreas: I will not remember her name. Forgive me.

Kit: It happened like this. Brel, the leader of the commune, said Aileen had spoken of me. Nothing more than that. He left it to me to make a move. I didn't for a day or two; I just began to notice how she behaved. She was no Chloe, no perfect little face, but that was reassuring. She was five years older and she'd lived more than I had. I never found out the whole story, but she'd had a rough few years before coming to the island. Her husband or partner had died. Drug overdose, I think.

Andreas: Or suicide, it can be hard to tell the difference.

Kit: Maybe. Aileen never told me what happened. On the island we all had daily chores and a rota. Each day we worked with different people. Back then I thought it was just to keep the group healthy, everyone speaking and working with everyone else. Later, I realised Brel arranged it to stop cliques forming and undermining his leadership. He needed to have control. There was something of that when he got Aileen and me together.

Andreas: Ah, a God complex?

Kit: I don't know if he wanted power, or feared everything falling apart. It did, eventually, but that was after I left. One morning, I was working alone with Aileen. We were digging up potatoes for the kitchen. We got talking. Soon we were telling each other our life stories, the bits we wanted to talk about. She knew more about me than I did of her, but she didn't ask the usual dumb questions. She wanted to read my poetry. Later, she told me she liked it and suggested ways I could improve it. I liked what she said. She thought the way I thought a poet should think. Sideways on, always alluding. I always ran straight onto the thing I wanted to say.

Andreas: My Elena would never tell me anything straight. Always left it to me to figure out what she wanted. I always knew, even when I thought I did not.

Kit: Maybe. But there was no alluding when it came to her getting what she wanted. That night Aileen and I shared a bed and we stayed together through the winter and into the spring. I was happy, for the first time in fucking years, I was happy... Sorry.

Andreas: You do not have to talk.

Kit: Life's a bitch at times. Hadn't expected it would be so painful.

Ω

Andreas: Did you hit it?

Kit: I think so. It dropped anyway. Wait here.

Lucky shot if I did. They don't usually get close enough. Luckily, Andreas and I were quiet and it wandered close. Can't hear anything so either it's dead or I missed it. No, there it is.

We have fresh meat.

Andreas: Then we need rosemary with it. There is some close by. I can smell it.

Kit: It's a young goat. An older goat would have been wiser. The meat will be tender. Andreas is picking rosemary for flavour. I've got it by the hind legs and I'm walking back with it. This isn't so bad. With two of us, I think we'll have the nets mended in two days. Then I hope the weather holds and we can harvest. Autumn won't last. We'll need to rig up something to get the carcass home.

What do you think, eh? It's a good size. Young as well. It will be easier eating.

Andreas: You shoot well. Is it heavy?

Kit: Heavy enough.

Andreas: We should carry it between us. Wait. I think I see… will this work? Tie it to this pole and we carry it between us.

Kit: Good. We can celebrate your arrival in style.

Andreas: I am surprised you still have cartridges for the rifle.

Kit: I'm careful with them. There, tied the legs. Not too heavy for you?

Andreas: No, and it will seem lighter for anticipation. I shall get an appetite.

Kit: Good. We should get going. Can't trust myself to follow the trail when it gets towards dark.

Andreas: And we do not want to get lost.

Kit: No. But I'd put the appetite on hold. Can't see me preparing this tonight.

Andreas: No? A shame. Tomorrow then?

Kit: Tomorrow, I promise.

Ω

Kit: We got back just before dusk. It's dark now and I'm sitting outside. Andreas is asleep.

I didn't think it would be so hard talking about Aileen. Nothing else I've remembered has affected me like that. I want to finish her story, and without Andreas's urging.

We'd got through the winter. My second winter, her first, and the fields were studded with flowers. We bred sheep for their wool and the lambs were already as big as their mothers.

I don't think Aileen had a death wish, but she often talked about crazy things she'd done, or fallen into, drugs included. I should have taken more care. Even if the air was mild, the sea was still cold from winter. I tried to dissuade her, but she was used to my caution and ignored me. Neither of us wore anything. No one cared. Clothing was only for warmth. I followed her into the water. She'd swum beyond the breaking waves. The seals, usually ever-present, had vanished as soon as they saw us. I remember swimming towards her. The cold was already sapping my strength. When I looked up I couldn't see her.

I tried to keep swimming. Looking for her. Couldn't understand how she vanished. I almost drowned. Luckily, one of the other residents found me collapsed on the beach. I never saw her again. Days later, her body washed up on one of the nearby islands. Autopsy said it was hypothermic shock.

Hope Andreas doesn't ask about her again. I don't want to tell that story twice. That winter with Aileen was the happiest in my life. After she died, my life on the island unravelled. Brel got paranoid. He feared people usurping him and had everyone informing on each other. Any breaches of rules, any misdemeanour overheard, had to be reported. When I told him I was leaving on the next boat, he stood there and screamed at me. Soon after, other members followed me back into the real world. I don't know what happened after that. Maybe Brel is still there.

Andreas is snoring away. I think he gets more tired than he lets on. Have to make sure he doesn't overdo it. That I don't give him more than he can do. I've gutted the goat. Need to do that quickly or the guts taint the meat. Tomorrow I'll skin and quarter it. Tomorrow will be a good day. Today has been a good day. I, too, am weary, but I'm sitting here. I'm unused to sharing time with another. Sometimes I just need to sit and think and listen to the waves and the wind in the trees. It's a clear night and the stars are shining down. The Pleiades are dipping to the horizon.

Still, I need to fish. May do that tomorrow and trust the weather holds for harvesting the olives. Andreas was too pessimistic. It won't take as long as he thinks. He won't want to come on the boat again, and it will be time alone. I'll leave him cooking the goat. He'll enjoy that and it's easy work.

Now, I must sleep. Goodnight my distant friend.

Transcript 033

Andreas: But we have all we need.

Kit: For today yes. And the next few days. I need fish for the winter. When the bad weather arrives.

Andreas: You are always planning ahead, tomorrow, next month, next year.

Kit: I'm good at planning. It was my job, once. Planning for the future.

Andreas: There is no future.

Kit: There's tomorrow and the day after. And next year.

Andreas: But later we eat goat, not fish.

Kit: Yes, I'll leave the goat to you. Don't let it burn.

Andreas: I know what I am doing. You go do what you want.

Kit: It's what I have to do.

Andreas: As you say. I think you are not so happy with this old man. You like creeping away by yourself.

Kit: Neither of us is used to company. It takes a while. Besides, I'm still recording my life.

Andreas: You are recording now?

Kit: I want to record as much as possible. It… it helps me make sense of things.

Andreas: You should believe in God, all this *wanting sense* of everything.

Kit: Don't you?

Andreas: I did once.

Kit: Why did you stop?

Andreas: Why? Why? Switch that damn thing off.

Kit: I'm going fishing.

Andreas: Go then. Leave me be.

Kit: This is harder than I imagined.

Ω

Kit: I don't understand why he gets so wound up. I don't expect him to be grateful to me; just to feel like he belongs here. Needs to share the place with me.

Anyway, left him on his own for the day. He has Wendy and the parrot for company. Taken the ropes in and raising the foresail. Won't go out far today. Sea's choppy and the sky's hazy. The weather's changing. Pushing off from the jetty. Foresail is catching the wind, pulling me round. Get on the tiller. Raise the foresail when I'm clear of the bay. Lot of wind noise. Hope you can still hear me.

The authorities released Aileen's body after the autopsy. She'd died of cardiac arrest brought on by hypothermic shock. She's buried in Thurso, far in the north of Scotland. Parents travelled up. Never heard Aileen speak of them so didn't even know their names. I couldn't tell for sure, but I don't think things were good between Aileen and her parents. Her mother spent the whole time with a scarf over her head, as though hiding from the weather, hiding from everything. Her father looked at me with something between dislike and distrust. There wasn't much to say. The churchman had come to the monastery a few times, so he was a familiar face. Learned from him that Aileen's parents blamed me for her death. Explained a lot. Whether I'd failed to save her or if they thought she'd gone into the water after me, I never found out. It was a proper, old-fashioned burial, coffin lowered into the ground. After the reverend said his words, Aileen's mother threw something down onto the coffin. It was a doll, maybe a doll from her childhood. They were grieving for the daughter they'd lost, not the woman Aileen had become. I wanted to climb down and get the doll back. It wasn't Aileen. It wasn't what the woman I had known, the wild woman who went swimming in the freezing sea, would have wanted.

But I didn't. I didn't want to make a scene.

That's all I want to say. Let me fish.

Ω

Kit: The boat's tied up. Caught seven sea bass, not so bad. Weather got livelier than I cared for and had a hard sail back. Fire's burning somewhere. Smells good. No sign of Andreas. Wendy is standing under a tree.

Wendy!

The robot's scanning. He's seen me.

Wendy, where's Andreas?

The robot's physiology is incapable of shrugging, but I swear that's what it's doing.

Wendy: I have no information, Kit. Wendy shut down to wait orders.

Kit: Why would Andreas set a fire and then disappear? There's something else as well. The smell of cooked meat. Maybe over-cooked. I'd follow my nose, but I'm keen to get the fish inside. Andreas isn't in the house. It's silent. Leaving the fish here a moment. Going outside again. Smell is strong. Heading towards a fire pit. Andreas has been cooking. Doesn't smell right. Poking around. Charred meat. Can't eat this.

Andreas! Where are you?

I'd half-expected some sort of disaster with the goat, but now I'm worried for Andreas. Is he asleep, or worse? Has he wandered off?

Wendy, find Andreas.

Wendy: Why?

Kit: Never mind why. Look for him, then report to me.

Wendy: Complying.

Kit: The robot's ambling away, which is as fast as it can travel. I'm going inside again. Andreas's bed is empty. Day's warm. Can't leave the fish much longer. Gutted them on the boat, but need to salt them to preserve them. Spreading out the fish and rubbing salt into them. Right inside the cavity. Andreas's absence is bothering me. I'm not concentrating.

Damn. Leaving these. Going outside to look for the old fool. Hands are filthy with fish. Running up the slope behind the house. Vantage point there, can see the whole area around the house. Got it. There's something white showing behind a tree.

Andreas! Is that you?

It moved. Bloody old fool. What's he up to. Circling round within the trees. Andreas is sitting with his knees under his chin. Face like a stone.

What are you doing here? I was worried for you.

Andreas: Nothing.

Kit: Did you cook the goat?

Andreas: Thought you would be back sooner. I fell asleep. It is ruined.

Kit: I saw.

Andreas: Not all of it. We would not eat all of it. Saved some. Dried goat meat lasts for months.

Kit: That's good. I've fresh fish.

Andreas: Not so good as baked goat.

Kit: No.

Andreas: And does not go with rosemary.

Kit: No, it doesn't.

Andreas: What does that damn robot want?

Kit: He's looking for you. I asked him to look for you. I was worried. Wendy, Andreas is here. You can stop looking.

Wendy: Any further orders?

Kit: No. You can shut down.

Andreas: You worry about me? What good is an old man?

Kit: We're all old men. Come.

Andreas: You do not mind about the goat?

Kit: I don't mind as much as you seem to. You're not the first to fall asleep while waiting for something to cook. Times I've been lucky not to burn the house down. Woken by the smoke alarm.

Andreas: I wanted to cook it the old way, in the open.

Kit: So I saw. It's okay. Fish isn't so bad.

Andreas: Hard getting old. Harder than you know.

Kit: Do you want to talk?

Andreas: It does no good. Does your friend need to hear an old man complain?

Kit: No.

Ω

Kit: Sitting outside again. Andreas is snoring, but it's not that keeping me awake. Tired enough to sleep through a herd of elephants snoring. Everything aches but I'm here, slumped over, my back to the timber supports of my house, and staring out to sea. The wind's picked up and there's a storm flickering out beyond the horizon. Hope it stays there. High winds will damage the olives.

I'm talking now because I miss being alone with my thoughts. And I'm worrying about Andreas. If he fell asleep when I left him to cook the goat, how can I trust him with anything serious? And reacting the way he did, like a child hiding from its punishment. Did he think I'd be angry? Or was he just ashamed? Tomorrow I'll finish mending the olive nets. The day after we start to harvest. Tomorrow will be easier on my own. Won't have to take things so slowly just for his benefit.

Transcript 034

Andreas: Where are you going?

Kit: To finish mending the olive nets.

Andreas: Alone?

Kit: There's not enough work for two of us. Besides, we waste time talking when we work together.

Andreas: Waste, you call it. Hear that, robot? He wastes time talking to me, but he takes you.

Kit: The robot can carry stuff. It's stronger than you or I.

Andreas: And it does not talk.

Kit: No.

Andreas: And what do I do here? What do you want me to ruin?

Kit: It's not like that.

Andreas: It is. Do me the courtesy of not lying to my face. You wish you had left me on my island.

Kit: Please. Don't make this hard. I came here to be alone. I'm not used to company.

Andreas: You have forgotten how to be companionable. You are friend to no one.

Kit: I can work alone faster than if you're with me. I can walk faster as well. It's easier this way. There's music in the house. Listen to anything you want. And you've got all your books. I have to go.

Andreas: Then go.

Kit: I'm going.

We're out of his hearing now. I know this makes sense. Wendy: I have instructions.

Wendy: Attending.

Kit: You will no longer take orders from Andreas.

Wendy: Andreas has not ordered me to do anything actionable.

Kit: Maybe not. But if he does, tell him you have to ask me first.

Wendy: Can Wendy respond to Andreas at all?

Kit: If he asks for something, you can reply. But don't act on anything he tells you to do. He's not himself.

Wendy: Do not comprehend. Andreas is Andreas. Kit is Kit. Wendy is Helpmate.

Kit: Andreas isn't always rational. We can't trust his judgement. He might do something foolish or ask you to do something foolish. So until I say otherwise, you will not act on anything he says or asks you to do.

Wendy: Wendy would not know right from wrong?

Kit: Not always. I can't trust him. That's all it is.

Wendy: Then Wendy will no longer accept orders from Andreas.

Kit: Thank you.

Wendy: Scenario.

Kit: Go on.

Wendy: If you are unable to help yourself and Andreas instructs me then failure to act on his order may place you in danger.

Kit: If I cannot help myself, then, and only then, you take orders from Andreas.

Wendy: Updated.

Kit: Hope it never comes to it, though.

Wendy: All scenarios must be considered. Kit may be unwell. Overheat warning. Cannot maintain pace. Precautionary shutdown imminent.

Kit: Bugger. Then stop here.

Wendy: Thank you. Apologies.

Kit: So much for plans.

We've stopped for thirty minutes. Wendy's CPU had got a bit too warm. My fault. The faster Wendy walks, the harder the CPU has to work to maintain his balance. Walking takes a lot of processing power. I was impatient and eager to prove a point. We'll go on presently.

Where was I in my life story? Give me a moment to think.

I was thirty-six the year Aileen drowned. I was now a failed gerontologist, a failed poet, and a failed Buddhist. I'd also failed at being a lover, or at least I'd failed at being marriageable. I bought a house in Herefordshire and retired to the country. The place had never had much to keep young people and I don't think the Barren had changed it much. Tried to join in with social things, but soon realised I was happier by myself. That changed when an ex-army instructor started a survival course out in the Welsh forests. Joined up, figuring if I wanted to avoid ending up in one of my own facilities, I'd need some basic skills. Learned bushcraft from him, but I drew the line at anything involving automatic weapons. Some on the course didn't share my concern: their survival would come at any cost. Maybe I just knew I could buy somewhere I wouldn't be troubled. Or maybe I knew about being shot. So –

Wendy: Notification. Cooling cycle now completed.

Kit: Good. We'll get going.

Wendy: Further notification…

Kit: I know, I know. We'll walk slower.

Herefordshire. In the forest I learned enough bushcraft to make a shelter and skin a rabbit and cook it. I'd also given real thought to where I'd want to see out my old age. Climate, terrain, resources, have a massive effect on survival and quality of life. Far north is too damn cold and I never wanted to plant another potato in my entire life. Greece was the natural choice. I told Mama of my plans that Christmas. Can't recall ever seeing her so happy. She told me not to wait too long as she wouldn't be around forever. I didn't tell her that she and I wouldn't be sharing a house. What I'd liked about Orkney was living on an island. On an island, you're in control; and there are many Greek islands. There were also many old rich people looking for a bolthole in paradise, but I had something most of them didn't: Greek citizenship.

But I'm getting ahead of myself. And I'm talking too much. Want to smell the air for a while.

Ω

Kit: I've spread the last of the nets out on the flat ground in front of the old outbuilding. Sitting on a stool and dragging the nets over my knees. It's rough and easy work. Won't win a prize for neatness. Tomorrow we'll spread these out beneath the trees and start picking. Quickest way is to physically shake the whole tree, or a branch of it, and the olives drop. Andreas will have plenty to keep him busy. Wendy's going through the grove picking up any rocks and bit of branch that might snag the nets. Don't want more holes in them.

Going to say more about those survival courses in Herefordshire. Owe a debt to the guy who ran them. His name was Ray Folger. Maybe twenty years older than I was. Big guy. Tattoos everywhere. Ex-SAS, he said. There was another man there, much younger. Also ex-army. Supposed to have been a mercenary as well. We only knew him as Frank. There were twenty of us in the group. Mostly men, a few women. I was one of only a handful that had never done anything like that before. Luckily, Ray wasn't inclined to ask people questions. That suited me. I managed to stay anonymous for quite a while.

Every meeting there'd be a tutorial, usually indoors. Then Ray drove us into the forest in a truck and we'd put it all to use. Sometimes, the tutorial happened in the forest. Several times we were given a map and compass and had to find our way out of the forest. But that wasn't what it was all about. As Ray always said, survival is teamwork. A team has a much better chance than someone on their own. The first rule of survival was to build your team. Never absorbed that lesson. But we were a strange team. Most wanted basic survival knowledge: how to make a fire; build a shelter; gather or hunt food; straightforward stuff. Others wanted more than that. They looked to the ex-mercenary and formed a group apart. I remember one saying to me that whatever I learned from Ray, it counted for nothing if he had a 7.62 cartridge and I did not; then he pulled it out of his pocket to show me.

I said he didn't have a gun. He said he didn't need a gun today; this was Herefordshire and I was no threat. But Frank would get him a gun anytime he wanted. I believed him. Then –

Wendy: Notification. Task completed. All obstructions removed.

Kit: Thank you. Don't step on these nets. Shut down until I need you again. I'll be another hour.

Wendy: Complying.

Kit: I always worry he'll get his feet caught in the nets and lose his balance. No longer certain I can lift him up again. He's backing off.

On second thoughts. I'd sooner just do this and talk about Ray another time. Should sit in the shade and breathe. This is a beautiful place. Turning off.

Transcript 035

Kit: High cloud has taken the edge off the sun this morning. It will be a good day for working. Setting a slow pace up to the olive grove. Don't want a repeat of yesterday and the robot overheating. Also, no need to tire Andreas. The day will be hard enough anyway.

Andreas: I can hear you muttering.

Kit: Just recording my observations. The weather is good.

Andreas: You were not talking about the weather.

Kit: I'm taking it easy on this trail. No sense in getting tired before we do anything.

Andreas: May we talk as we walk, or is that tiring also?

Kit: We can talk. What do you want to talk about?

Andreas: You were telling me last night about men with guns: surviving, maybe using guns to survive.

Kit: What of it?

Andreas: It interests me to know why a man would pick up a gun and buy his survival at such a price.

Kit: I didn't. Never owned anything more powerful than my rifle.

Andreas: Not saying you did, but some did. We had robbers, like in the bad old days.

Kit: Bandits?

Andreas: Like little armies. Not good. Many died.

Kit: It will be a long day today.

Andreas: I know.

Kit: Be truthful, do you think you're well enough to work?

Andreas: I think so. I hope so. I intend repaying you.

Kit: You don't have to.

Andreas: We all owe to each other. I am old, much older than you. Remember that. I do not always remember it myself. In my heart, I am still young.

Kit: I've never asked how old you are.

Andreas: I am seventy-nine. There was a girl, you know. When I was fifteen. I might have had a son, or a girl, I wouldn't have minded.

Kit: I'm sorry.

Andreas: I was not the only one. You were saying about guns.

Kit: The instructor didn't teach us much about guns. If you were into that then you asked this other guy, Frank. Never knew his last name. If you had the money, he could get you anything you wanted, so long as you could carry it. Unlike those who were friendly with Frank, I'd been shot. It put me off. Plus, I knew I could buy myself protection if I needed it.

Andreas: In Greece there were plenty of guns. But few had anything to steal. And those who had something to steal had guns.

Kit: Surviving isn't about power, it's about knowledge.

Andreas: And buying an island just for you.

Kit: I didn't buy the whole island. How did you survive, at first I mean?

Andreas: People always need dentists.

Kit: The guys who wanted guns were no good at making friends. Mostly they'd scare people or acted like they wanted to be alone.

Andreas: Did you want to be alone?

Kit: No. Not then. I wanted to be anonymous, but that's not the same thing. I wanted to be ready.

Andreas: For what?

Kit: This.

Andreas: Harvesting olives?

Kit: Ready for the end, the last decade or so of humanity. When everything, near enough, is broken and everyone's waiting for death.

Andreas: Ah, yes. But life is more comfortable with something to fuel the lamps.

Kit: It helps.

Andreas: So how did this end?

Kit: In death. We had a survival week in the Welsh forests. More remote than anything we'd yet done and it was winter. There was an accident. Two people fell off a mountain path. One was killed, the other died later. Turned out Ray hadn't got any licenses for training or running a survival course. After that, everyone drifted away. Last I heard, Ray had died of blood-poisoning from a squirrel bite. Ever eaten squirrel?

Andreas: No. Never thought it worth the effort of catching them.

Kit: It isn't. It's steep along here. Might be better to save our breath for now.

Andreas: Agreed. But someone taught you how to use a rifle. That much I have seen.

Kit: Another time.

Ω

Kit: We've spread the nets out beneath the trees. We'll take them one at a time. Shake the olives onto the nets.

Andreas: I know how to harvest olives and so do you.

Kit: I was just giving a picture, for whoever is listening.

Andreas: No one is listening. If there is anyone, they have better things to do than listen to old men talk about olives.

Kit: This will be hard work. Do you think you're able?

Andreas: If I am not, then tell me before I kill myself trying.

Kit: Remember, there's no rush.

Andreas: No rush, he says. Listen, whoever you are, this is a harvest, a dozen things may go wrong.

Kit: A dozen?

Andreas: Many things. The weather may turn. A storm when the olives are ripe and ready to fall. Wind scatters them. Bruises them so they do not keep.

Kit: Then we should not delay. This tree first.

I'm swinging on a bough. It's old wood. The new stems grow up from it. The bough gives and the new growth swings. Olives are scattering into the net. Pulling the net so the olives gather together.

Is this how your wife's family harvested?

Andreas: They had machines. Shook whole tree. Faster and easier. You should have bought one of them instead of that robot. Cheaper too.

Kit: Maybe.

Andreas: This is too hard for me. If you have no mind, I will milk the olives. Slower, but easier for me.

Kit: That's okay.

I carry on shaking the branches. Andreas is going to the next tree. He's climbing into it and running his hands down the new stems. Spilling the olives into the net below.

The cloud is thinning and the sun catches the back of my neck.

I probably ought to stop talking. The olives fall and roll into the folds and creases of the net forming green veins. Switching this off.

$$\Omega$$

Kit: Surprised at you. Thought you'd weaken.

Andreas: I know my pace. It is you who slowed. You should try milking the olives.

Kit: I was taught that shaking the trees stimulates them. They grow more vigorously.

Andreas: Old wife's tale. My way is easier. That is important at our age.

Kit: It's also slower.

Andreas: That is true. But I think this weather will hold for a while. And you need your strength for pressing them.

Kit: Grab the corner of the net. Get them out of the sun. They'll dry as they are.

Andreas: These crates have seen better days.

Kit: As have I, But they'll do. Bring that edge round. Easy.

Andreas: You should get rid of the twigs and leaves.

Kit: I know. I will. Just… not now.

Andreas: As you wish.

Kit: I'm thinking ahead. We've a few more days of this. Gets harder every year.

Andreas: Growing old has that effect. But we live with it or we grow angry with ourselves.

Kit: You were angry.

Andreas: True. I have you to thank for making me less angry. I shall die happier for that.

Kit: Sooner you didn't. Not till the olives are in.

Andreas: I will do my best to stay alive until then, but old men cannot always keep their promises.

Kit: What does that mean?

Andreas: Matters are not mine to control. We should stay here tonight, save walking each day.

Kit: I do, usually, when I'm picking olives.

Andreas: So why not now?

Kit: Thought you'd prefer a proper bed.

Andreas: I do not mind. Sleeping here is better than walking each day. The robot can carry what we need, save us wearing our bones.

Kit: You admit a robot is useful.

Andreas: All brutes are useful. It is peaceful here, away from the sea. I grow tired of the sea. Don't you?

Kit: I haven't yet.

Andreas: But you are not as old as me.

Transcript 036

Kit: Servos again. We set out earlier today. Wendy's following with overnight things. It makes sense to stay overnight. We can spend more time harvesting and with less effort.

Andreas: What happens if robot breaks down or falls over?

Kit: He can radio me.

Andreas: Truly?

Kit: This recorder will pick up his signal.

Andreas: I am impressed.

Kit: You're making fun of it?

Andreas: No. Having one of those things would annoy me, but I admit the robot is useful. The parrot I like. I have been teaching it to swear in Greek, but it is not learning so quick.

Kit: I'm sure it will, in time.

Andreas: Time, you say; as if we have so much.

Kit: We've time enough.

Andreas: Maybe.

Kit: You want to hear the next part of my story?

Andreas: Why not? It passes the time.

Kit: I bought a farm.

Andreas: You, a farmer?

Kit: Farm owner. I employed a manager.

Andreas: In this English place you were before?

Kit: No. Spain. Cheap land out there. Labour from North Africa and India.

Andreas: So what went wrong? Did someone die, or someone try to kill you? That seems to be the way with you. Surprised I have not tried to kill you.

Kit: No one died. At least, not directly.

Andreas: That sounds promising, and yet not.

Kit: I needed to do something with my life; both keep myself busy and be of use. Figured people would always need food. Unfortunately, we had bad luck with prices and weather. One year drought. Next, floods. The year of the floods, we lost sixteen workers, some to drowning, more to dysentery. Spain was bankrupt even before the Barren. By this time there was no welfare system and not much in the way of state infrastructure: roads were terrible, police and local government corrupt. There was a reason the land was cheap.

Andreas: But what was it like there? Remember, I have lived nowhere but Greece.

Kit: The people had grown hard, those I dealt with anyway. They'd suffered too long. The church held society together at the start, but people had drifted away from it.

Andreas: But this is not your story. This is history, no? Whoever is listening will know all this. What happened to you?

Kit: Ah. You're saying this should be my story, not the story anyone can tell.

Andreas: That is what I meant.

Kit: I can't.

Andreas: Why not. I overheard you before.

Kit: It feels wrong. It's as if I'm confessing. When you're listening, it's like an interrogation, or an interview. I feel guarded.

Andreas: Please yourself.

Kit: Don't take it badly.

Andreas: I am not. I think I understand. If I spoke of my life, I should not want you listening, maybe judging, asking lots of questions.

Kit: Exactly. I'll do it later. Maybe tonight.

Andreas: When I am snoring and you cannot sleep.

Kit: Yes, probably.

Ω

Shaking the trees is hard work. Harder than it was yesterday. I'm still sore across the back. Maybe Andreas has the right idea; harvest slower, but with fewer aches to pay for it.

Andreas: What you are saying?

Kit: That your way might be right. My back hurts.

Andreas: You will learn.

Kit: Perhaps. Still worried about the weather changing. I think speed while it stays good.

Andreas: Please yourself. I shall not change.

We should think about pressing what we have gathered. They will dry, even out of the sun.

Kit: Can't afford the delay. We press on. Rain now would be a disaster.

Grabbing hold of a bough and shaking violently before letting it spring up. The fat olives fall and roll across the netting. Moving round the tree, pushing and shoving. Got a rope for the higher branches. I throw it over them then swing on it. How many more years can I do this? Five? Ten? Could I do this at Andreas's age? I doubt it. Time when the body packs in. Don't think about it. Don't get distracted.

Ω

Kit: We've eaten. Some of the goat Andreas burned was edible, and there's bread. I brought wine, also. Or rather, Wendy brought it in the cart. It's my own wine. Drinkable. Wild grapes. He's shut down for the night and Andreas is sleeping. I'm outside the old outbuilding, sitting with my back to the wall. It's chill, but not too cold. Night's always colder in the hills. I've found a lavender bush and crushed a stem between my hands. Love that smell. Looking at the stars, it reminds me of that night near Kastoria all those years ago.

I'll try and say what needs to be said about the farm in Spain. For a long time, I blamed the manager. His name was… but there's no need to name names. I blamed him, but it wasn't his fault. Call him Pedro and hope I don't offend his memory. He hated the Africans. Wanted me to employ Spaniards, but the African migrants were twenty years younger than most of the locals and worked longer hours. Most of the work was manual; fuel prices meant machinery stood idle. The only thing we needed fuel for was the water pumps. Either the local Spanish didn't want the work, or if they did, they didn't work fast enough. I should have promoted the best of the migrants, and sacked Pedro.

One morning, Pedro came to me with news. Said it was the *blacks*, as though that said everything. I'd grown tired of trying to get Pedro to see the workers as people. He drove me out to the barracks: men in one, women in another. There were no families. Two men were sitting in their compound beside their barrack. A third man lay on the ground between them. As we drew up I realised the third man was dead. Pedro said they only killed their own.

The two men sitting down got up and came to us. The dead man had tried to steal someone's woman. They wanted me to bury him. I asked who had killed him. The two men looked sideways and pleaded with me not to ask questions. The dead man knew what he was doing. This was how it was.

Pedro said not to ask questions.

I asked the dead man's religion.

He was Muslim. Muslim in name only one of them said. Good Muslim does not steal man's wife.

I asked Pedro to help me get the dead man in the truck. He looked disgusted with me, but he did help. Whoever killed him had left him without much of a face. Think he'd been beaten to death.

Pedro and I drove into town and arranged a funeral with the migrant office. I paid the costs. Stuck it for another six months before selling up. Chinese bought the farm for about what I'd paid and I was glad to be out.

It's late.

Transcript 037

Kit: The stones are grinding the olives into paste. Once the farmer would have used a mule for this. Now, it's just me, pushing this wooden beam round at walking pace. The beam creaks on its spindle. The stones rumble. It's noisy, but you can hear that.

Andreas is out picking, or milking as he calls it, more olives into duralene bags. This only the first stage. The paste will need pressing to extract the oil.

Wendy is too short to work the grindstones. The arm is above his shoulder height. Can't get his weight behind it. My beast of burden is useless for this and so I grind. The sweat's running down my back, but at least I'm out of the sun.

Andreas: Save your breath, you will need it.

Kit: Talking breaks the boredom.

Andreas: Suit yourself.

Kit: Andreas has left a bag of picked olives and taken another bag to fill. I don't think I can ask him to work the grindstones. It would kill him. It's half-killing me. Need to scrape the paste from the stones. Should be done quickly. Exposure to the air oxidises the oil. In the old days, it would taint the flavour but I've never understood if it reduces the calorific value. This is fuel, not cooking oil. It lights my lamps when there's not enough sun for the solar cells. Certain power in uncertainty. Scraping the paste into a drum. Then I'll pour olives onto the slab and return to grinding.

May as well talk to relieve the boredom. I left Spain with Chinese money in my account and drove north. French border guards wanted proof I wouldn't be dependent on the state and my travel plans. I told them, north to the coast and away. The guard warned me against Calais, saying the migrants had overrun the port, but Le Havre was still safe, then.

The guard post had a faded mural on the far wall. Blue flag with a circle of stars. I drove north. There was no ferry at Le Havre. The ship had broken down. Abandoned the car and chartered a fishing boat. Took me to Newhaven. There, I bought another car and drove to Herefordshire. The house was empty and cold. Damp had settled in its stones. I didn't care. I must have slept for two days.

Within a week, I was sick of the cold and the damp and making plans to leave. I'd got a taste for hot climes while in Spain, but wanted something familiar. Greece was the obvious choice.

With hundreds of islands, many of which were uninhabited, Greece had found a convenient way of propping up its broken economy. If you had money, you could buy an island. I wasn't rich enough to do that, but I was half-Greek and I had my fame which, for once, was useful. I also had youth on my side: most of the islands' younger generation had left to work abroad or on the mainland.

There were dozens of islands to choose, all struggling to hold on to the few people left. What persuaded me here, and not there?

Andreas: You are talking to yourself again.

Kit: Gives me something to think about.

Andreas: It is not getting any easier at our age.

Kit: You're bearing up, though?

Andreas: I can manage. Rather outside than in here working like a donkey.

Kit: Someone has to do it.

Andreas: You say that robot is too short?

Kit: Yes.

Andreas: You should build a walkway, so high. Then it can walk round and work the stones for you.

Kit: Maybe. Lot of work, though.

Andreas: Bah, you're not interested in my ideas.

Kit: No, that's not what I meant.

He's gone, taking the bag I just emptied. It's not what I meant at all. He looks tired, whatever he says.

I lost my place. Yeah… So I contacted the Greek Embassy in London. Got an appointment with an attaché. She was intrigued. Put me in touch with the Ministry for Shipping and Island Policy. Month later, they invited me to Athens, gave me a pass for an official flight. Turned out to be a military transport and none too comfortable. Took four hours. Ministry put me up in a government hotel. Spartan, but okay. Next day I saw the minister. His name was Thanasis Giannopoulos.

I can remember his first words: so you're the famous Khristos Zachariades. Please, come. This is a moment. Would you be so kind?

Didn't know what he meant, but he took me over to a window with a view of the city and the Acropolis in the distance. The infamous smog was no more as hardly anyone had money for a car and the air was clear. He got me to stand there with my back to the window and a photographer came in.

Giannopoulos asked if I approved the idea: I, the last man, and behind me the birth of civilisation, as the Greeks saw it. I humoured him. Next day the photo appeared in the Greek press and on the ministry's website. I couldn't complain. Now all of Greece knew I was there.

The photographer left and Giannopoulos showed me to a chair. He said I wanted to purchase an island. I said no, I didn't have that kind of money.

That was a mere detail, he said, and suggested I wished to invest in an island. That sounded agreeable. I didn't want to live like a hermit.

Then he asked me why. It was hard to answer the question. Wasn't a homecoming as I'd only spent a few months in the country, and none of that on an island. Nor could I'd say that I'd tried everything else and failed.

So I said it was the climate and because I won't feel like a stranger here. I had my name.

Giannopoulos said it was an honour the last man ever to be born was a Greek; even a half-Greek. He asked about my natural father. I admitted I knew nothing, though it was possible I was a full Greek. English by habit, though.

He agreed I did not behave like a Greek and said it might present difficulties and opportunities. Some communities would resent me as foreigner; others might welcome me for the same reason, or accept my name as my passport to join them. The problem, he said, is the youth of the islands have left and those remaining are ageing fast. The people are set in their ways and won't leave. It's not easy to provide for them. He suggested I had expertise in geriatric provision. I said it was a long time ago and my experience wasn't relevant to their needs.

He asked what I could offer an island. I said money, investment. He seemed pleased. Turned out he was worried I'd had an idea of being welcomed just because of my fame. I hadn't. Giannopoulos explained that while the ministry had some interest in my situation, I would need to approach the civic authorities on the islands and he handed me several sheets of paper filled with names and addresses and a letter of introduction.

He admitted the letter might not count for much as most of the islanders had a low opinion of the ministry. Resources were scant and there were many islands. The list contained names and addresses of the mayors for all the islands, starting with the poorest that were most likely to be interested in an investor.

The ministry's generosity couldn't extend to a personal guide, but I was welcome to stay another month at the hotel. During that time I should arrange meetings with as many on the list as I wanted.

Then the meeting was over. Giannopoulos shook my hand and said it was a pleasure meeting me.

And that, my friend, is how I returned, or arrived, in Greece.

I'm scraping the olive paste into the drum. Need a break. Haven't seen Andreas for a while. If he's any sense, he's taking a rest.

Transcript 038

Kit: It's only now I'm away from the grinder that I've realised how loud the damn thing is. Can't hear the breeze, or any birds. Everything's silent. I'd lean against the wall of the outbuilding but the stones are too hot. Full sun today. Shade would be good. Shade and fresh air. Can't see Andreas, but if he's climbing trees to harvest the olives I'm not surprised. I'll hear him soon enough. Damn. That's ridiculous. Walked in a half-circle. Too long pushing the grinder round. That's better.

Taking a lie down by this tree. Good to sit down, if only for a moment. Switching you off for a bit.

Ω

Kit: Bad feeling. Sun's shifted, so I've been asleep over an hour. Too many nights sitting up listening to Andreas snoring. Where is he? Can't believe he's seen me sleeping and not said or done anything. Not like him to be generous. On my feet, walking through the grove. Branch has come down. Must have been last night. No. That's not right.

Andreas!

There's something under the branch. I'm running. No breath.

Christ. Andreas. Can you hear me?

He's alive. Breathing. Bloody fool must have brought the branch down. Landed on him. Got to get it off. No. Check his airways. Tongue's not choking him. Bruise on his head. Nose is bloodied. Arm's caught up in the branch. Don't think it's broken. Get him free. Now, heaving. It's heavy. Trying again.

Got it.

Andreas? Andreas, can you hear me?

Breathing sounds rough. Chest is barely moving.

Wendy! Wendy, come here. Urgent.

Robot's better at medical stuff. Can't tell whether Andreas fell and knocked himself out, or if he's collapsed and then fallen. Need to take a pulse, but my hands are so calloused there's no feeling in my fingers.

Wendy!

Wendy: Complying. Cannot proceed faster.

Kit: Why now Andreas? Why now?

There's something not right with his face. Drooling from the side of his mouth. What does that mean? Stroke, I think.

Facial paralysis. Wait. Checking his pupils. Turning his head out of the sun. One pupil's is dilated. I think that means a stroke. Don't have my torch on me. Wait; turning his face into the sun. Pupil doesn't change. Must be a stroke. Aspirin, yes? You're supposed to give aspirin. But how?

Wendy!

Wendy: Almost there.

Kit: Give me a diagnosis. A man is unconscious and one pupil is larger than the other. What does it mean?

Wendy: Optical pupil?

Kit: What? Yes, yes, his eyes. One pupil larger than the other. Come here.

Wendy: It is typical symptom of a stroke. Is Kit unwell?

Kit: It's Andreas. He's fallen. Need you to take his pulse. Here. I'll hold his arm. You take his pulse. Can you detect it?

Wendy: Pulse detected. Weak and irregular.

Kit: What are you doing? Why are you taking so long?

Wendy: Allowing one minute to elapse.

Kit: But surely –

Wendy: I have the result. The pulse is 74 but erratic.

Kit: What should I do? Advise me.

Wendy: Stroke victims must be kept warm. Aspirin may help as it is an anti-coagulant. Must be taken orally.

Kit: Have to move him inside. It will get cold tonight. Help me carry him. Take his feet.

To look at him, you'd think Andreas weighs nothing. Not so.

Can you walk faster?

Wendy: No. Balance is compromised. Proceeding fast as possible.

Kit: Wait. Take his legs over your shoulders. Sorry, Andreas, doing all I can. Yes, that's it. Now, Wendy, hold

Andreas's legs so they don't slide off your shoulders. Can you walk more easily now?

Wendy: Yes. Balance improved.

Kit: Good. We'll take him to the shed with the olive press. I'll make a fire. You will... no, cancel that. You will go home, get aspirin, and return immediately. No delay.

Wendy: Cannot carry out order. Insufficient daylight to maintain battery charge. Cannot travel at maximum speed.

Kit: Please God. Then do it as fast as you're able in the circumstances. Do not incur any delay. Understood?

Wendy: Understood. Once returned, will Wendy be required to do additional work before opportunity to replenish batteries?

Kit: No. But I must have the aspirin soon.

Wendy: Unconscious patient cannot take aspirin.

Kit: We must hope he recovers consciousness. Put him down by the wall. Now, go.

Wendy: Optimal speed and endurance requires Wendy to charge batteries before departure. Permission to delay.

Kit: What?

Wendy: Optimal speed requires battery fully charged.

Kit: Can't you recharge as you go?

Wendy: Tree cover will prevent optimal recharging. Calculate remaining here will optimise speed. Do you dispute calculations?

Kit: No, no. Okay, stay until you've recharged, then leave immediately.

Wendy: Will comply.

Kit: How long till it's dark?

Wendy: Calculate two hours. Permission to shut down all non-essential processes to minimise charging period.

Kit: Yes, yes.

The robot is sleeping. Need to get firewood for tonight. Trying to run, but my legs won't do it. Dragging the branch Andreas was under. Fitting. Saw and axe in the outbuilding. Use them to prune the trees. Should be piles of pruned wood from last spring. God, I feel wretched. I failed. Should have realised something was wrong soon as I got away from the olive press. Andreas had looked tired. Wasn't his usual self.

Sorry, I can't talk now.

Ω

Kit: I'd switched you off. Had a moment by myself. Telling myself that a stroke is just a stroke. It happens. No one's to blame. Think I've enough wood to get us through the night. Have to be careful though. Don't think I can do much more. Everything hurts. Wendy's gone. Won't see him for a few hours. Hope I've got the instructions right. Maybe it would have been better to put Andreas in the cart and help Wendy drag him home. Maybe quicker. But riskier. Path is uneven in places. Risk of the cart tipping. Hope this is for the best.

Andreas hasn't changed. Breathing's still shallow. I'm trying to take his pulse, but I can't feel anything. First stars are showing. Sky's clear. It will get cold. I've wrapped Andreas in olive nets. Should think of myself as well. Fire's lit. Need to sit up to tend it. Be a long night. Will he live? And if he lives, what then?

Seems wrong, but if I keep talking I'll stay awake. Better than sitting and worrying. Getting myself comfortable. Cold now the sun's gone. Sorry Andreas if this is boring.

I had the names from Giannopoulos. I made calls, trying to narrow the options. The first few places thought I was fascinating; the last-born man on their island, but it was soon clear I wasn't rich enough for them. They wanted a big investor, someone who could rejuvenate their island. I'm not sure the person they wanted existed.

Then I came here. The mayor, Stavros Diamantidis, met me at the ferry terminal in Marathias. The port was then a town of fifteen hundred, but most were thirty years older than I was. He was short, but well-built. Intelligent and shrewd. He said the island's children had gone. They were abroad, tending the aged in Germany and Switzerland. They're like beggars, he said. Like blacks.

I didn't correct his racism. I needed friends. Luckily, Diamantidis wasn't looking for a messiah to save the island. I think he mostly wanted someone to talk to and complain with. Someone who was an outsider and not looking for someone to blame. I liked him.

The next day after a night at a lousy hotel, he showed me a map and pointed at a bay on the east coast, saying that if I wanted to be a castaway then it was the perfect spot. The bay was surrounded by a protected area. Diamantidis said it was a wildlife reserve, but as we were now the endangered species it was a trifling problem. Wildlife would soon have half the damn island. And one day all of it, if God doesn't preserve us, he said.

Diamantidis, I soon learned, was not an optimist. The day after, he drove me out along the coast road, stopped at a bridge and then walked me through a valley to the shore. I asked him who owned the land and he looked furtive. I thought it might be state-owned, which meant I'd need to go back to the ministry in Athens. But no. Diamantidis was selling me family land. He shrugged and said that as his children had no interest, he may as well sell it to me.

I should check on Andreas. I wish Wendy were back.

He's still breathing. Skin's cold. Not surprising if his pulse is weak. Building up the fire. God I'm tired.

Transcript 039

Wendy: Notification. Have returned with aspirin.
   Kit: What? Where?
   Wendy: This is the olive grove. Are you unwell?
   Kit: No. No. Must have dozed off. What did I ask you to get?
   Wendy: Aspirin.
   Kit: Yes. I remember. Can you take Andreas's pulse for me?
   Wendy: Power reserves critical. Attempting compliance but shutdown imminent.
   Kit: Forgotten he's out of power. Christ it's cold. Moon's up.
   Wendy: Report. No pulse detected. Shutting down. Battery recharge commences at dawn.
   Kit: What? No. You can't! What do you mean: *no pulse?*

Transcript 040

Kit: Andreas died… No. Get this right. My friend Andreas Alexandris died last night between midnight and four. Cause of death… suspected stroke. Can't be certain. He passed away without recovering consciousness. Don't know if I made his last days happier or not. I made him a promise, and though, God knows, no one would know if I failed to keep it, but I would know and perhaps you also know. For now, that's all I can say. Rigor mortis has set in. No idea how long it will last. Maybe a day, maybe longer. Need to bend his legs to fit him in the cart so Wendy and I can get him home. I think that would have amused him: even in death, he's stubborn. Carried him… well, dragged his body away from the outbuilding and left it in the shade. Can't abandon the harvest and I can't work with Andreas just lying there. I know it seems wrong. Needs of the living outweigh those of the dead.

$$\Omega$$

Kit: Is this how we honour the dead: by recalling what they said and acting on it? I remembered Andreas's idea of getting Wendy to work the olive mill. He can't push because he's too short. But I've rigged up a simple harness and he's dragging the beam round. Seems to be working. He calculates he can last six hours before he needs to recharge. That's more than I can manage. I'm shaking olives off the remaining trees. The day's cloudy and cooler than of late. I think the weather's turning. The mountains always have more cloud than the coast, but this is more than I've seen since late winter.

Talking takes my mind of things. I miss Andreas, but more, I wish I didn't have this responsibility on me. So much to do. Need to get Andreas buried within a week. No more. Try not to think of all that. Late in the year for sailing.

Let me describe this, in the here and now. The nets spread beneath the tree. The tree. Let me describe that. I've pruned these trees, and before me, Aristotelis Voulgarakis pruned them. The trees are old, much older than Aristotelis was, but only the trunks and the lower branches are old. Each season's fruit comes from new growth so most of the branches are whip-thin and sprout vertically from the old wood. I thrash them with a long pole and the olives fall, along with leaves and dead wood. The trees are taller than the pole can reach. I could climb up in the branches – that's what Andreas was doing – but won't take the risk. There'll be enough without doing that. My back aches from wielding the pole. The fallen olives roll into the creases in the net. I tread carefully to avoid crushing them.

Diamantidis. Yeah, Stavros Diamantidis. He died – no, I won't get ahead of myself. I told him I'd be in touch. He looked at the ground shaking his head.

English are polite. Never straight, he said. Then he's waving an arm about, saying I didn't like what I'd seen. I said it wasn't that. Giannopoulos had given me a list and I intended to work through it. Diamantidis said I needed to trust my instinct. I wouldn't find a better place to make my home. He was right. That little bay had everything. The island had everything I needed and, more to the point, I felt like it wanted to accept me.

But I was English and I had that list. In fact, the next two islands I called at were so dispiriting that two weeks later I was back with Diamantidis. The deal had to be approved by the local and regional government but it never bothered anyone that Diamantidis was mayor and vendor. Still, Greek law moves slowly and it was six months before I could stand on the shore and call it mine.

Before that, Diamantidis introduced me to the people of Marathias and Servos, holding the introduction party at his villa above the port.

It was a brilliant spring afternoon. Diamantidis had advised me to arrive by car, but I walked up from my hotel near the fish dock in the old town. My relative youth and white skin marked me out and the local press had made a story of my arrival.

Halfway up the hill I saw a man following me. He shouted if I was the Englishman. I stopped and said I was half-Greek.

I read about you, he said. You rich Englishman come to help us poor Greeks.

I denied it.

So you rich but not help us? What half of you is Greek? You look English to me. English bad as Germans. They destroy Greece.

I said Stavros Diamantidis had invited me to the island. He wasn't impressed. Diamantidis was a crook. I should ask anyone who had dealings with him. They'd all say the same. Did he even own what he sold me?

I couldn't answer that, but I'd my own suspicions concerning Diamantidis. I put my head down and kept walking. He followed me for a bit, then offered a curse and asked who my mother had fucked to get a half-breed bastard.

Diamantidis greeted me at his door. I said I wasn't wholly welcome on the island and told him about the man who followed me.

He said I should have taken his advice and driven. On the street I'd see things I may not wish to see. People were angry. I said they were angry everywhere.

The difference was, they'd been angry here a long time before the Barren.

Diamantidis didn't pay attention to them and neither should I. Next time, I must take a car.

But I wanted to get on with people. Wasn't going to spend the rest of my life in seclusion.

Diamantidis warned me. I was a rich man. People were in hard times. They might go back to their old ways, take me, slice off an ear, demand ransom. Then what?

He had a habit of giving advice as though it was an order. He'd been elected twice as mayor so someone was happy with him.

I asked who'd pay a ransom for me. He said he pitied me.

That's enough for now. Life could be worse. I'm not sure how, but I'm sure it could be. I'd rather be alive than where Andreas is.

Pouring olives into a bag for taking back to the press. There's been thunder up in the hills, but no rain. I don't think it will rain. Not yet, anyway. Later, I'll get firewood for tonight. I'm turning you off for a while.

Ω

Kit: It's night. Wendy's on standby, though I don't think I'll need him between now and morning. I'm sitting by the fire and unpicking the stitching on some duralene sacks. I was using them for the waste left from crushing the olives, as it makes good fuel for the fire, but I'll make a shroud for Andreas. Leave the sewing for morning when I can see. It will keep the flies off him. More respectful as well. First part of my promise.

Transcript 041

Kit: It's early, not long after dawn. Or as near to it as you get in the mountains where the horizon pushes the sun long past its usual rising. I've harvested more olives and left Wendy to grind them, though he reminded me working indoors means he cannot recharge. Suspect his batteries are weakening. Must ask him to run a diagnostic.

Sewing while my hands are still able. Be too worn by the end of the day even for this rough work. Laid out Andreas's corpse. Rigor's gone and he looks almost peaceful. This is his shroud. No illusions about decay and he must be buried soon, if for no other reason than he'll become a source of contagion. A shroud will keep the flies off.

Shouldn't call the corpse a *he*. This isn't Andreas. Andreas has gone. Habit's hard to break.

Sewing requires little thought: just enough to stop me running the needle in my thumb. I can talk as I work.

Diamantidis had ideas about what the last-born man might choose for a house. He, or his family, also owned a construction company. Diamantidis, if not an outright crook, knew how to make power work for him. His villa looked like a concrete Delphi, so you can guess what he proposed for me. We disagreed. I wanted something simple I could maintain. He didn't understand why a rich man would work when he could pay others. I pointed out that when I was old there would be no one left to pay. I needed simple durable, or easily repairable materials: wood, stainless steel fittings. Stuff that would last or be repaired with hand tools.

I was channelling Ray Folger: *depend on nothing you cannot repair or replace*, that was one of his bits of advice. Reinforced concrete was beyond my abilities. Also, I can tell the workmanship and quality of material in wood. Paint on concrete can hide anything.

But Diamantidis didn't understand. This was my first visit to his villa. He swept a hand round to encompass everything in sight. You, he said, might live in a palace, yet you choose a wooden hut.

I called it a cabin. I was thirty years his junior needed to plan for when there was no one to labour; only old men and old women.

Diamantidis shrugged and said no one on the island would build such a house. He meant, no one would gainsay him and build it. He'd turned to include those standing near us. All immaculately dressed, the women looking twenty or thirty years younger than their real age, the men with hair dyed black contrasting with their sun-worn faces. Like Diamantidis's miniature Delphi, they were living in a sham. The nearest people to my age were the Albanian staff hovering in the corners of the room. If young Greeks served Germans and Swiss, young eastern Europeans served old Greeks.

Except no one was young. I had turned forty and, despite appearances, was the youngest in the room. It wasn't till halfway through the evening I realised the Albanians were dressed like children.

A woman approached me. I couldn't guess her age. She was slender and dark haired, but her cleavage was immobile as furniture and when she spoke her upper lip barely moved. She said I should take more care of myself. It did not do if the youngest man in the room did not look his age. She knew a man who could work wonders, so she said. Those little grey hairs, those lines around your eyes. He would set them right.

I smiled. I'm smiling now. The desperation, vivid on their painted faces, was tragic but it amused me as much as Daniel's robot sister had once scared me. I declined. I would always know how old I was, as would anyone who recognised my name.

She protested that I made all of them feel old by comparison. I said it couldn't be helped. I could not avoid my age.

I stayed that night in a guest apartment at Stavros's villa. He joined me for the first part of the evening and we drank raki until I saw he was filling my glass and not drinking his own. I remembered something my mother said: never trust a Greek who doesn't drink. The conversation turned back to plans for my home and all the things I would need, which somehow matched everything Diamantidis had, only this time at my expense. I dipped a finger in the vodka and drew an A on the table, saying that would be my house.

Diamantidis was mystified, so I showed him on my phone.

He said no Greek would build such a thing.

I said no Greek would have to. It came ready for assembly. Then he saw the company was German.

It didn't go well. He would forbid it. I pointed out it was my land now. I didn't need his permission. I had Giannopoulos's backing and in a wildlife reserve, all planning was subject to the ministry.

Diamantidis threatened me: saying whatever I built, I would still need to eat.

That was the last time I was a guest at Diamantidis's villa, but nothing came of his threats. Having invited me to the island, he didn't want to lose face by turning on me. Besides, he'd overstated his influence and several locals were happy to do subcontract work on the building.

Sewing finished. Andreas has a shroud, though the duralene's harsh and the colour's faded to a dull grey. I'm all out of linen. Sit for a while and rub oil into my hands before I try and sew him into it. Then, carry on harvesting the last of the olives.

I've talked myself out. Need some silence around me.

Ω

Kit: Twilight. Last of the sun has gone and the stars are showing between the clouds. Don't think it will be so cold tonight. Death robs a man of all dignity: Andreas soiled himself. Couldn't stomach washing him, and besides, without disinfectant it isn't safe. State my hands are in it wouldn't be hard to catch something nasty. Did my best for him. Shroud will protect him for now. Awful business. Not ready for sleeping yet. Head's too active, even if the body is tired.

Wendy?

Takes a moment for him to respond.

Wendy: Attending. Instructions?

Kit: Play cards with me.

Wendy: Is it essential?

Kit: It is.

Wendy: Cards are a pastime, not a necessary act.

Kit: Sometimes trivial things are necessary. It doesn't matter that you don't understand. Come. It won't be for long.

Wendy: What level do you wish me to play?

Kit: Three, level three. I want a chance, but not too easy.

I'm dealing. Wendy can hold the cards, but can't deal them. Lacks the dexterity. I'm not doing great either. Cards are so old I might know each by its creases and worn edges. But where's the fun in that?

Handing Wendy his cards, face down so I can't see. Wendy barely looks at them before laying a queen. I reply with a seven. Wendy lays a two. I cannot reply and Wendy wins the hand.

Will we finish the olive picking tomorrow?

Wendy: Too many variables to calculate.

Kit: Am I a variable?

Wendy: Humans are always variables. Chief variable is the weather.

Kit: Thank you.

Wendy: Why do you thank me?

Kit: For saying I'm more dependable than the weather.

Wendy: That is not what Wendy said.

Kit: It was close enough.

Wendy: Conversation between humans is unlike that between human and robot.

Kit: What do you mean?

Wendy: Frequently I did not understand what was said between you and the late Andreas.

Kit: Humans often misunderstand each other. I wouldn't let it worry you.

Wendy: It does not worry me. Andreas is silent now.

Kit: Excuse me a moment. Don't look at my cards. Need to make water.

...

I'm standing under a tree. The robot couldn't care less, but I'm still English in many ways. *Andreas is silent now* is one way of putting it. A voice silenced makes a robot's existence less confusing.

You didn't look at my cards, I hope.

Wendy: You gave instruction not to.

Kit: And you cannot break an instruction.

Wendy: There are circumstances –

Kit: I know the circumstances.

Wendy: I have report.

Kit: Now? But nothing's happened.

Wendy: Incorrect. Data informs the deceased are no longer capable of movement.

Kit: Correct. Mostly correct, I think. What do you mean?

Wendy: I saw Andreas move.

Kit: You can't have.

Wendy: Movement observed in visual and infrared spectrum.

Kit: Bloody hell. Andreas? Andreas! No, don't be a fool. He cannot not be dead. Where, where did he move? What moved?

Wendy: Heat signal detected. Furthest point from the fire

Kit: It's still there?

Wendy: Yes.

Kit: Christ. What is it? Oh, Jesus! That's horrible.

Wendy: Heat source gone. Movement ceased.

Kit: I saw it! I fucking saw it. Sorry old friend. I should have thought of this.

It was a rat. Bastard's chewed through the duralene. This is obscene. Not going to see what it was doing. Can't bear to. This... this alters things. This is wrong.

Wendy, how much power do you have left?

Wendy: Sixty percent. Endurance twelve hours at current operating demands without factoring solar recharging.

Kit: Good. Sit here tonight and guard Andreas. If that rat or anything else appears, get rid of it. Here, use this.

It's an olive switch. Nice and springy. Wendy's swinging it tentatively.

Wendy: Calculate agility of small mammals renders this ineffective.

Kit: You don't have to flatten them with it, just scare them away.

Wendy: Understood. Success cannot be guaranteed.

Kit: New plans. Tomorrow we leave for home with Andreas in the cart. You must be fully charged before we begin back.

Wendy: The olives will spoil unless they are pressed tomorrow.

Kit: Can't be helped. No rat is chewing on Andreas. I made him a promise.

Wendy: Must promises be kept to the dead?

Kit: Always.

Wendy: But there is no reciprocity. The dead cannot return the promise.

Kit: I can't explain it. Guard Andreas as though he were I and still alive. I must sleep.

Wendy: Did I win at cards?

Kit: You won. Now, let me sleep.

Transcript 042

Kit: I don't know if this is the right thing. Dozen trees not yet harvested and the fruit will drop and rot into the ground before I can return. Of the olives I – that Andreas and I – harvested not all are crushed and of those that are, only half have been pressed to extract the oil.

Andreas would laugh at me sacrificing the harvest, or most of it, to fulfil a promise he likely made in jest. Nothing he said ever struck me as the words of someone who cared for posterity, or cared for a grave that in a decade, at most twenty years, no one will be alive to visit.

Yet I will do it.

And there are practicalities. Ugly facts. Rats are the least of it and I must act fast before things become impossible. Once home I'll decide what to do. I can pack the corpse in salt, salt from his home – the irony – which will preserve it for a time. Even if I do so much, I'll lose the best part of three days here and I've already lost days. But I'm drawn to sail immediately and bury him as he wished. The weather may decide for me. I haven't laboured so much in years, yet it's strangely exhilarating; I have purpose, albeit a purpose that makes no sense.

I've things to do and talking will only interrupt my thoughts.

Ω

Kit: Everything can be left as it is here. What oil I've pressed is stored and won't spoil. The harvested olives and the paste will dry out, but will serve as fuel as they are. The dozen unpicked trees won't matter. Time to leave.

Wendy. Put this around your shoulders. It's a harness so you can help carry Andreas into the cart.

Wendy: Andreas is dead?

Kit: Of course.

Wendy: Then what is Andreas?

Kit: This body is Andreas. It doesn't matter. I call him, it, Andreas out of habit even though Andreas is no more.

Wendy: Do not comprehend, but will accept corpse is Andreas to avoid confusion.

Kit: Thank you. I'll tie the sling around his… around the corpse's feet. I don't think you'll be able to grip the duralene. It's too slippery.

Lifting up Andreas's feet and tying the end of the sling around his ankles. If I hold his shoulders we should, Wendy and I, get him into the cart. I could do it on my own, but it would take all my strength and I don't trust the stitching to hold on the shroud.

Are you ready, Wendy?

Wendy: Incomplete instruction.

Kit: We lift Andreas's corpse and place it lengthwise in the cart. That means I go to the front of the cart and you at the rear.

Wendy: Understood.

Kit: One the count of three, we lift. One. Two. Three. That's it. Swing round to your right. Now follow me. Match my pace.

How can one old man be so heavy? In life you'd think a breeze would blow him away. Now he weighs like wet sand.

Wendy: Estimate thirty kilos. Within design capabilities. Confirm poor grip on this material.

Kit: Now sideways, over the edge of the cart. Set him down gently. Good. Done.

Wendy: Bio-hazard alert. Detect low-level risk of disease due to contaminated meat.

Kit: Andreas isn't contaminated meat, but thank you for the warning.

Wendy: Recommend attention to hygiene.

Kit: I'm dealing with it.

I should be careful. Lots of cuts and abrasions on my hands. Haven't fully healed since rebuilding the saltpan. Olive oil is a passable decontaminant and it's all I have.

Now, we go home. You haul the cart, but go slowly. Don't want to risk overturning the cart. I'll steady it from behind.

Wendy: Understood. Battery levels at eighty-five percent.

Kit: That's enough?

Wendy: Estimate five hours mobile endurance.

Kit: Remind me when we get back. Need you to do a diagnostic on your battery life.

Wendy: Will comply.

Kit: Now, we walk.

Ω

Kit: We're halfway. I'm taking a rest. Wendy's standing in the open recharging his batteries. Hard work. Cart's wider than the path, what there is of it, and with Andreas's weight, plus the tools and other things I need back home, it keeps getting stuck on roots and rocks. Wincing every time the carts jolts or lurches. Andreas is beyond pain, but it's awful. Wendy has said that Andreas cannot hear my apologies. I'm seeing gaps, whole absences in his awareness I'd never noticed. I told you old men talk to themselves and it seems we talk to the dead also. Though surely almost everyone I've spoken of is now dead? Perhaps not: Hannah was my age, Joan only a year older. Chloe... who knows what happened to Chloe. Daniel, no, I think he would have ended it by now. Jack Regis sailed on a boat. Everyone at Diamantidis' party, with the exception of a few of the Albanian and Moldovan staff, is surely dead.

This is too depressing.

Wendy?

The robot straightens up.

Wendy: Attending, Kit.

Kit: Have you recharged?

Wendy: Atmospheric conditions impeding optimal recharging. Reserves sufficient at current usage to reach home with safety margin.

Kit: Good. We need to go. Take up the harness for the cart.

He's climbing up from the ravine. Takes a moment to reach me. There's something childlike in its movements.

Can't you go any faster?

Wendy: Optimising pace for battery endurance.

Kit: I'm impatient. Andreas got on with things – I think he was more impatient than I am. Waiting for the robot seems to take an age but can't have Wendy lose power before we're back. My fault anyway. Should have maintained this path better. I can walk it easily enough, but manhandling the cart is slow and exhausting.

Wendy: Please attach harness.

Kit: Good.

Buckling the harness across Wendy's torso. He's taking most of the weight. I stop the back wheels fouling any roots or rocks. When the cart's lightly loaded, it just bounces over them, but with Andreas's weight, it can't. Besides, it's no way to treat the dead.

Advance, Wendy. Notify if your power reserve drops below fifteen percent before we've reached home.

Wendy: Will comply.

Kit: If necessary, I'll drag the cart myself the last part of the journey. Hoping it doesn't come to it.

I was guessing about Diamantidis' friends all being dead. Diamantidis died of a heart attack five years after I arrived here, though there were rumours he was poisoned by a business associate. The others… Some I recall dying here, but most left when the Ministry of Geriatric Provision evacuated everyone over sixty to the mainland. Most went willingly as facilities here were bad, but a few holdouts ran to the hills.

Eventually, the last islander died and I inherited.

What am I to do, Andreas? Stay here, or inherit your island? You've got salt and I haven't. I'll pack you in salt later. I think you'd appreciate that; it's your salt. But then what? What am I to do?

Wendy, you tell me. What am I to do? Stay here or take myself to Andreas's island?

Wendy: Insufficient data to advise. Please give defined parameters.

Kit: Cancel question.

He's right, though. Too little information to understand question. God I miss Andreas. Wendy. Stop.

Wendy: Is Kit unwell?

Kit: I am as well as can be expected. I'm an old man, Wendy. Things hurt.

Switching you off. You don't need a commentary. Later.

Ω

Kit: Wendy's shut down to conserve power. Every muscle aches, but my head is on fire. Sitting in the dark talking to Billybones. He's only interested in pinenuts.

Billybones: Nuuuut!
Kit: Here.
Billybones: Aaandreas!

Kit: Andreas is dead.
Billybones: Aaandreas?
Kit: Bastard's taught the parrot to repeat his name. This is too much.
Billybones: Nut.
Kit: Say thank you.
Billybones: Thank you, who?
Kit: He's giving me the eye
Billybones: Nuut?
Kit: You've got one. Don't be greedy.

If I got drunk tonight, would that make it better or worse? Worse, I think. Tempting though it is. And I'll feel terrible in the morning and I can't afford that. Need to think clearly.

Billybones: Dead!
Kit: What?
Billybones: Doesn't know it!
Kit: Nut. Have all of them and shut up.

Left the parrot and walking down to the shore. Sit a while and listen to the waves. Missed them. Can't see the Pleiades tonight. Might be too late in the year, or cloud cover. Can't tell. Not that it changes anything.

Transcript 043

Kit: Switching this on. Damn… got salt on it. This shirt is filthy. Laundry… well, some things haven't been washed in a while. That noise is Mozart's Requiem, played loud. I'm shouting so you can hear me above the music. Sacrilege, but if I shout, I don't have to think about what I'm doing.

Andreas… Andreas is two days dead. Several more days, two at least at sea, before I can bury him. I've refrigeration, but can't risk contaminating food. Next best thing is salt,

Andreas's salt, and olive oil. Vile work. Bandaged my hands, but the salt still stings. He's skin and bone. There's no give in his flesh. Cut the clothes off him. This is by far the worst thing I've ever done. Bet the bastard's laughing somewhere. That's enough. I want to hear the music.

$$\Omega$$

Kit: Hands are red-raw. Washed them in fresh water. Fingers like claws. Try to sew Andreas back into a shroud later. Found some clean duralene. At least, cleaner than the old sacks he was in. Burnt those. No dignity in death. Suppose my father's death was the same. Someone undressed, wiped the shit off his backside, washed, dressed him. Same for all. Almost all. I'll rot where I drop, already decided that. No grave. No marker.

Except for this recording. It's a sort of memorial. A record I was here.

There was something I meant to do.

Wendy. Come here.

Wendy: Attending.

Kit: Run diagnostic. Maximum battery endurance and recharge efficiency. Compare to default values.

Wendy: Endurance fifty percent manufacturer's specification. Recharge efficiency, sixty percent. Endurance in line with number of recharge cycles. Recharge efficiency compromised by physical deterioration of solar panel.

Kit: Recommendation?

Wendy: New battery pack will improve endurance. Manifest indicates two in storage. Solar panel not replaceable without service engineer.

Kit: Can the scratches be polished out?

Wendy: Possible, but would only yield marginal improvement.

Kit: I thought so.

Wendy: Information. Transfer of data to spare chassis unit provides optimal improvement.

Kit: I know. Not yet, eh. I'd miss you.

Wendy: Do not understand. Spare chassis identical to Wendy. Transfer of memory means no loss of functionality.

Kit: But I'd still miss you.

How does one explain things to a robot? Every scratch, every dent reminds me that he... that it and I have endured here. But I can give him a new battery pack.

Remind me how I fit a new battery pack.

Wendy: Installed batteries must be exhausted before removal to prevent risk of sudden discharge. Reserve power sufficient to run instruction program to assist replacement of components. Notification. New batteries will require one charging cycle before maximum efficiency attained. Recommend battery replacement earliest tomorrow to maximise solar period.

Kit: First thing tomorrow it is. Exhaust your batteries overnight then shutdown by the storeroom.

Wendy: Will comply.

Kit: If only humans were so simple.

Ω

Kit: I'm sewing Andreas's new shroud. Kneeling, bent over, as if in prayer. Hard on the shins. Should get up and put something under my legs, but I can't make the effort to get up and find something. Barely holding the needle steady. Can't knot the twine without it slicing into my hands and opening old cuts and sores. Telling myself I'll never have to do this again for anyone. That's all I can think of. It feels like penance.

Sewn down one side and turned around his feet. Using a block of wood to force the needle through the duralene. Can't hold the needle tightly enough to push it through. If Wendy needs a complete charging cycle then I can't sail tomorrow. I need him to have maximum endurance. It's another day of waiting. Reluctant to take the robot with me but it's a long climb up to the ridge to bury Andreas, and I'll keep my promise in full, even if he never expected me to. Need to protect Wendy from saltwater damage.

Why couldn't you have wanted to be buried at sea, eh? Struck a hard bargain for this salt. Bet you're laughing at me. You, who no longer made plans, ask this of me. But you were good company.

We need more music. I can't get up.

Music command. Monteverdi: Vespers; Sixteen-ten.

The wonder of machines. Now listen while I sew. As for you, Andreas, hope you'll appreciate this, you old barbarian. Might not be your thing, not raucous enough, not alive enough for you. Too bad.

Ω

Kit: The wind picked up late afternoon. This is late in the year for adventures. I'm walking down by the shore, listening to the waves and the wind in the stone pines. I say walking; I'm hobbling really, just trying to keep everything from seizing up. Every year gets a little worse and harvesting olives is hard work. Glad he gave me the idea of hitching Wendy to the olive mill. I'd never thought of that. Next year, wherever I am, there will be olives to harvest. Don't trust my electrics over the winter. Oil, though, oil is dependable.

Does it really make sense to move my life to Andreas's island? I need salt, yes, but here I've electric power most of the time, even if it isn't wholly reliable. I can think about that this coming winter. Make up my mind in the spring. For now, sail to his island, bury him, and return. If I could delay that until spring, I would, but the dead do not wait on us and there's no way of preserving his corpse over winter.

Wind's cold and I should be going in. Hope the weather clears tomorrow. Or better, the day after, for then I'll be sailing.

Transcript 044

Kit: Nothing is simple, or as simple as it should be. Unpacked a new battery unit for Wendy. It's bulky and heavy and sealed in a layer of plastic which has yellowed with age. This plastic layer baulked me. Instructions say no metal tools, so a knife is out. Probably because metal might short the battery. But surely there's no charge after all these years. Maybe there's another reason, but the instructions are clear. Reading them is like a glimpse into another world, a lost world of production lines and engineers. No metal near the battery unit. So, I'm reduced to picking at the packaging with what's left of my fingernails. It's slippery and – damn!

That hurt. It's brittle as well and I've cut my finger on a sharp edge. Have to find a blade that will cut this. I must have something.

Ω

Kit: This is working. Plastic will cut plastic, after a fashion. Getting the last of it off. Hope Wendy appreciates my efforts. It's strange to see something looking so new. Everything else is worn. This is pristine – the plastic casing white and unmarked. I'm staring at it and smiling. Shame it will be hidden behind the panel on Wendy's back.

Leaving the protective strip across the terminals for the moment. Wendy's rear panel unscrews. I have a key. The first bolt's unwinding. Keeps unwinding. Why isn't it...? Oh. Captive bolts. I did the same thing five, maybe more years ago. I should be able to remember. Two more bolts on this side, three on the other. There's a dust seal. Have to be careful with that. Might be brittle. Heat and sun over the years. Last bolt's loose. There... No, panel's sticking. Be careful. Prying it loose a bit at a time. Should be doing this under cover, I suppose. Gust of wind could pick up dust. But Wendy needs to be in full sun to recharge quickly. Experts didn't think of everything.

It's coming. Good. Putting it aside.

So, Wendy. This is what you're like inside. Surgeon Zachariades here. God knows, enough surgeons have poked inside me. You, that's you, listener, haven't heard about the last one: appendicitis a year after I arrived here. Damn lucky that time. Surgeon was ancient, came out of retirement as a favour. The new Greek minister, I forget his name, Thanasis Giannopoulos had been replaced, the new minister arranged for drugs to be flown out of Athens. Chloe had tried to kill me for who I was; now someone saved my life for the same reason. It evens out.

No appendicitis here, just a tired battery. Checking the diagram inside the rear panel. Battery unit mounts inside an alloy frame. Damn, this thing is heavy. Need a bigger key for the bolts. One's missing. One out of eight. I remember these aren't captive. Wendy still has a loose bolt rattling around in one of his feet. Never seems to trouble him, but not ideal. I need to turn you off and concentrate. Don't suppose this is interesting anyway.

$$\Omega$$

Kit: Wendy has a new battery. Rear panel's back on and the seal is okay. Reserve power is minimal, but enough to trigger a notification he's recharging and will be fully charged, assuming present input remains the same, in five hours.

Not a cloud in the sky today.

The sea is almost calm as well. Only a slight movement out beyond the bay. It would have been better to be sailing while the weather is good. But Wendy wouldn't have had sufficient power to help me bury Andreas. So I lose a day. Can't be helped.

I need something to eat.

Ω

Kit: These tomatoes have suffered in the last few days. Not been here to water them. No matter, they're almost over for the year. Picking enough to make dinner. I have olives, last year's preserved in brine: I've yet to gather any for eating from this year's crop. Also pasta, the ideal preserved food, and dried sea bass. I'll make an open fire and boil the pasta. Can put the fish in it to soften it up.

The tomatoes taste of summer.

I remember Diamantidis watching the lorry unload my provisions. Almost all of it tinned and dried goods. The German contractors cleared a track to the site from the coast road. There wasn't depth to land a big enough ship, and a helicopter was impractical. The track's long overgrown. My provisions were one of the last loads to come down it. Diamantidis, hunting rifle in his arms, watched the unloading and turned to me with a smile, saying he and the rest would know where to come when they were starving. I smiled back, though I knew he would expect me to be charitable. Most of the island men had rifles. Hunting was a passion for most of them. I recalled Ray Folger and his assistant, Frank. The one who knew how to get an automatic rifle, one for hunting bigger prey than wild goats and songbirds. I said nothing to Diamantidis, but I kept my stores locked.

There was no showdown. As I said, the authorities evacuated most of the islanders. Those left found enough to live off. They left me alone. Then I was wholly alone.

Gathering thyme and rosemary. I like the smell of them on my hands. Later, I'll crush them with a little oil and stir it into the pasta.

Ω

Kit: Wendy's new battery indicates seventy percent charge. He's moved twice now to follow the sun. I think all will be well. If the battery holds a bigger charge and the solar panel is compromised, he'll need a longer recharging time. Can't see a way of avoiding that. Just have to try and keep the panel as clean as possible.

Water's boiling. Dropping pasta into it and breaking up the dried fish. Flesh stays in big flakes without breaking up into mush, and the water draws out most of the salt. Been a few days, maybe more, since I ate properly. The last good meal I ate, Andreas cooked.

Don't get maudlin.

No wine. Maybe this evening when I've nothing left to do. After eating, I want to see to the boat. Need to make a harness for Wendy. He'll have to stay on deck. Too bulky to get him through the hatchway. Need to keep the spray off him. Andreas, also, will go on deck. Can tie him to the cabin roof. Hope to make Marathias tomorrow evening. Sky's clear and the sea's calm.

Draining the pasta and stirring in the tomatoes, olives, and the pesto. Pasta and fish will warm everything through. It's salty, but palatable. Feel okay. My hands are healing.

Ω

Kit: Sitting with a glass of wine. Night and I'll be in bed soon. Stars shining but no sign of the Pleiades. Can't recall the date they set. Wendy could tell me, but he's shut down for the night. Battery charge peaked at ninety-seven percent, which is good enough. He claims this will improve after a few charging cycles. Done everything I can on the boat. Prepared as I can be. With a fair sea, we will all arrive safely or at least in the condition in which we left.

A drink to my health, and to yours. Goodnight.

Transcript 045

Kit: I've woken early. Before dawn. Sea's calm and silvered in the half-light. Too early to do any work; still too dark to see. Walking above the wave line, making for the rocks at the end of the bay. Filling time. Keeping warm in the chill air.

Wendy confirms the Pleiades are below the horizon. It's no longer, according to the Ancient Greeks, propitious for voyaging. Though the number of Greek shipwrecks in the Aegean suggests they didn't know everything. Besides, weather patterns have changed over the millennia and old lore no longer passes.

But it's late in the year and this calm is deceptive. And besides, if this calm persists I won't be sailing anywhere.

Climbing up into the rocks. Trees shadow me from the dawn. Birds are awake and calling. You can hear them. Clouds far out to sea are catching the light below the horizon and glowing pink.

Ah! Breath of wind on my face. More promising. Sit here until there's enough light to work by. Not hungry yet. Expect I will be presently. Need my strength today. Marathias by nightfall. That's the goal. And nightfall comes earlier now.

Days are shorter. And if I can't make Marathias? Plan. Can't risk lying offshore. If there's cloud, I'll be blind. If the wind drove me towards the shore I wouldn't know until it was too late. Or I could be blown offshore and wake to see no land. No. Have to come inshore while it's still light, find what shelter I can and rely on the anchors.

Sun's rising now. First point of light above the horizon catches on the waves, making a silver ray. Clouds are flushing golden. Breeze again. Sun's shaking up the air. Tops of the trees dip into it and birds show in the branches against the dark blue sky.

Need to let Billybones free before I go. He won't wander far.

$$\Omega$$

Kit: I'm standing beside the boat. Wendy's climbing on board. I need him to help carry Andreas aboard. He's ready now. It's like watching someone perform a dangerous trick.

Can your balance sensors cope?

Wendy: Yes. But optimising balance causes significantly greater power use.

Kit: I understand him. It's tiring to stand and move on a deck constantly shifting under your feet.

It's only temporary. You don't need to be mobile when I'm sailing.

Wendy: Adjustment completed. Settings optimised.

Kit: Good. Sorry old friend. Wendy, take Andreas's feet. Carry them the way you did last time. Can you do that?

To my relief, he slips the sling around his neck and stands. Andreas's feet come off the ground. Hoping the stitching holds on the shroud.

Move backwards and we'll carry him on board.

Wendy: Information confused. Is this package animate?

Kit: Animate? No, of course not. It's Andreas. Andreas's corpse. Just carry it onto the boat.

Wendy: Complying.

Kit: I'm stepping aboard, one foot first. The boat dips under my weight and shifts away from the jetty. The stern rope halts it, but Andreas is straddling two feet of water, as am I. Don't be squeamish, damn fool. I'm grabbing Andreas by what I think are his shoulders. His head's lolling within the shroud and resting against my knee. Damn, this is taking all my strength.

Wendy. Put the feet down and come here. No, the other side. Quickly.

He's complying. Losing my grip on the duralene. Quick. Take the weight. Extend your arms beneath him. Good. Hold him. You have his weight?

Wendy: Approximately forty-six kilos.

Kit: Good.

Didn't need to know how much he weighs, but that sounds okay. Relaxing my hold. Andreas isn't plunging into the gap between the boat and the jetty. Nor am I. Stepping aboard.

There, old friend. We didn't drop you.

Wendy. I have Andreas now. Go back to his feet. We'll carry him to the roof of the cabin. Careful now. That's it. Proceed.

We're moving slowly across the deck. Not much space. Ducking under the boom.

This will do. Lift Andreas onto the cabin roof. That's it. I'll tie him down so he doesn't move.

Wendy: Andreas no longer capable of movement. Andreas is inert object.

Kit: It's complicated. Sometimes this thing wrapped up in sailcloth is just a thing. Sometimes I think of it as Andreas, even though Andreas is gone and this is just his body. I know it confuses you, but that's how it is.

Wendy: Will interpret either to refer to package.

Kit: Good. Though it wouldn't make Andreas happy to be called a package.

Wendy: Is Andreas unhappy?

Kit: No, he's not unhappy. But we have to respect what he would have wanted were he still alive. This is still Andreas, understand?

Wendy: It is illogical.

Kit: You will have to accept that. Is everything Billybones says logical?

Wendy: Billybones is incapable of comprehending speech.

Kit: Oh, he comprehends well enough. He knows how to ask for a nut. Humans also aren't always logical.

Wendy: Am aware of human illogicality as a concept but in practice it creates uncertainty.

Kit: Well, I'm sorry. We'll both have to live with uncertainty. Now. Thank you. Task concluded.

Ω

Kit: Finally, we're underway. Still in sight of home, but we're sailing. Tied Andreas down and Wendy shelters in the lee of the cabin with an old sail wrapped round him. We tried, but he's too broad in the shoulder to fit through the companionway. Only way would be to lower him vertically and I've nothing to do that with. He's protected from everything except a wave breaking over the stern.

Wendy, turn off your motion sensors. Need you to conserve power. Remain on standby.

Wendy: Complying.

Kit: It's later than I'd hoped, but things always take longer. We've a decent following wind, so there's still a good chance of reaching Marathias by nightfall. I know the mooring well enough.

Andreas, you're going home, just as I promised.

Wonder if he believed I would do it. Like to think so, but he was a realist. Perhaps he knew I was a romantic. Truth is, I've failed too many people to fail another.

Damn. Boat's too lively. Need to take in sail. Don't want to ship any water on deck. Not with Wendy sitting where he is. Switching you off. Need to be careful.

Ω

Kit: How long is it since I spoke? Lost track of time. Still daylight. Made good time, but the last two hours have been brutal. Taken all my energy, and seamanship. Wind's been steady, but the sea's turned on me. In a following swell the stern rises and endlessly pitches the bows into the back of the previous wave. Like riding a seesaw. A seesaw that sometimes stops dead or slews sideways. Easy to lose the foresail in these conditions. If that happens then all hell breaks loose. Boat spins in the water like a top.

But it didn't happen. Everyone's safe. Water's sheltered here and I can see Marathias. Won't be going ashore tonight.

Wendy. Respond.

There was a lot of spray came over, but not too much water came aboard.

Wendy?

Wendy: Running diagnostic for possible damage. Will report.

Kit: That's worrying. Can't see him because I've wrapped him in sailcloth. Ah, something stirred. Think he's okay.

Wendy, wave to me.
Wendy: Complying.
Kit: Good. Any damage?

Wendy: Some water contamination in lower limbs. Core systems unaffected. Request fresh water to prevent corrosion from salt spray.

Kit: Remind me again after I've got the boat moored. Is that the only damage? What about battery levels?

Wendy: Battery at eighty percent. Power drain minimal.

Kit: Good. Better than I feared.

As for Andreas, the sailcloth kept the worst of the spray off and I don't believe he has moved at all. So far, apart from myself, we're all doing well. If you don't hear from me again today it's because I'll be asleep. Was going to tell you about building my house, but it'll wait.

Ω

Kit: Jesus! What's that? Pitch black. There it is again. Someone's on deck. Some thing. Where's the torch. Dogs. It must be. Christ, they're after Andreas.

Hey!

Got a stick. Best I can do. Climbing on deck. Night's cold. Clothes were wet so I've slept naked. Got a blanket round me.

Hey! Get away.

Three of them. Retreated to the bow.

Wendy. Alert.

Wendy: Attending, Kit. Instructions?

Kit: Guard Andreas's body. Don't let anything near it. Use force.

Wendy: What is nature of threat?

Kit: Pack of dogs. Keep them off him. Be careful. Don't trip on anything.

Found the boathook. Decent reach on it.

Get away! Go on!

One's jumped off. Barking. Two left.

Get off.

This one's a brute. Trying to grab the boathook off me. No time for kindness. There!

That must have hurt. Vicious hook on this thing. It's backing away. No place for it to go, except over the side. It can swim for it.

Last one. Not so brave now. Turned and fled.

God I'm scared. And shivering.

They've gone, Wendy. Scared them off.

Wendy: Why are dogs attracted to boat?

Kit: They can smell Andreas I expect. To them, he's meat.

Damn. I'm shivering. Not enough sleep. And it's cold. Clear night. Starlit.

Dogs again. Up on the fishing boat. The steel deck amplifies sound. Eyes flashing in the torchlight. Wendy, can you see them?

Wendy: Thermal vision identifies four dogs. Unknown breeds.

Kit: Size?

Wendy: Three approximate to a German Shepherd. One smaller.

Kit: Have your lower limbs dried out?

Wendy: Yes. All systems are optimal. Report significant power drain maintaining full alert.

Kit: Then shut down everything except audio and visual sensors. If the dogs return, alert me and protect Andreas.

Wendy: Will comply.

Kit: Andreas, you old sod. I think you're more popular now than you were alive.

Hey! Dogs.

Beating the stick on the trawler's hull. Like a drum. You can hear the noise. Why am I telling you? Damn but I'm tired. Tomorrow we sail on. Had wanted to stay another twenty-four hours. Wanted to check the boat after the beating she took today. But the dogs will come back tomorrow night and there might be more of them. Can't take the risk.

Need to get some clothes on before I catch cold. Wendy can take care of it for a moment. Switching you off. It'll be a long night and I'll only ramble. No sense wasting your time. German company built the house with German overseers and a few locals who preferred cash to following Diamantidis's orders, which were that the mad Englishman got no help. They had the frame erected in four days and the fitting out completed within a week. There. I've told you about building my house. That will have to do. Goodnight.

Transcript 046

Kit: It's morning. Later than I'd planned. Been light for a few hours. Got to sleep eventually. Dogs didn't return but Wendy's power reserves are depleted after standing guard all night. He's recharging now, but have to wrap him in sailcloth before we leave.

Why is everything so hard? Fate's been against me ever since the storm when I lost my salt. One blow after another. I'm too old for it. We are all too old for it! Do you hear me? We're too old!

Quiet, old man, you're shouting at nothing.

Ω

Kit: My father would have disapproved, English reserve and all that. He died in far worse pain than I'm in, and he had the pain of parting from those he loved. I've done that, piece by piece. No one left to cry over now. Andreas! Can you hear me you old bastard? Want to change your mind; burial at sea? No?

Please yourself. In death as you did in life. I'd drink a glass with you now. I'd drink you under the fucking table.

Wendy: Report concern for Kit's wellbeing.

Kit: You're concerned? You're not the one sailing the damn boat.

Wendy: Boat not sailing. Boat moored. This is Marathias.

Kit: Be quiet. That's an order.

Wendy: Complying.

Kit: I sometimes wonder if his programmer meant my tin man to always have the last word.

Boat's a mess. Didn't get to see to everything after mooring last evening. Too damn tired. Start at the bows and work back to the stern. Took a beating yesterday, as did I. With any luck, it's no more broken than I am. Though I'd relish an extra day here. But the dogs will be back tonight. Certain of it.

Can I throw you to the dogs, Andreas? No?

That's a shame. You'd be a piss-poor meal. All sinew and bone. Though the rat wasn't choosy. Sorry about that. Should have thought. Should have thought of the dogs too. Guess anything with a nose can smell you a mile off. Ah well.

Switching you off, my friend. Less excuse for rambling if no one's listening.

Ω

Kit: Nothing appears broken on the boat. I'd stay here another day, just to be certain, and to give Wendy time to recharge, but can't risk it. Don't like the weather either. Sea beyond the harbour is as bad as yesterday. At least the wind is from the right quarter. I'll make good speed. Eat something before I go. Sooner go ashore and make a fire, but no time.

Dried fish again. At least I've tomatoes, last of the summer's vine. Once I'm underway I won't be able to leave the tiller, not in this weather. Ever tried taking a piss while hanging onto a wild horse? It's something man was not intended for.

Ω

Kit: I'm softening the fish in a pan of cold water. Got ten litres, enough for four days. Always the chance of being blown out to sea or something vital breaking on the boat. Used two litres yesterday washing Wendy down. Water makes a cold, pale mush of the dried fish. It's salty and I've never got a taste for it, but it's palatable and full of protein.

Sometimes I could die for a decent coffee and slice of cake. The simple pleasures. Tomatoes bursting on my tongue. Sweet and drown the saltiness of the fish. Caught sight of myself in a mirror earlier. If I had any doubts I was fucked...

Still, Andreas must look worse.

Wendy, stop recharging. What's your power reserve?

Wendy: Fifty-eight percent. Fully recharged in another two hours.

Kit: Can't wait for that. Get back behind the cabin. Need to wrap you in sailcloth and get underway. What's the wind speed and direction?

Wendy: Twenty-five knots and gusting. North-north-west, veering.

Kit: Barometric?

Wendy: nine-six-seven, falling slowly. Indicates weather worsening.

Kit: I know what it means. We need to sail. Get in position.

Going to be busy. No time to talk.

Ω

Kit: Update. Two hours out of Marathias and in the channel between the islands. Boat's taking a pounding again. Worse than yesterday. One of the ropes holding Andreas to the cabin roof has come away. Can't see clearly from where I am, but I think it's forward on the port side. Poor bastard's sliding toward the edge of the cabin roof. Handrail there might hold him. Other ropes are holding. Could lash the tiller and go forward, but bad idea in a following sea. If a wave catches under the stern the boat can turn beam on; the sail gybes and everything goes to hell. Worse case is a capsize. Can't take the risk. It's exhausting and still a way to go. Need to get my weight behind the tiller, keep her steady. Ha! What weight? You're skin and bones like Andreas. Still. That's better. Everything hurts. If needs be, I can drop the mainsail from here and then go forward. Be a bastard getting it up again, but the boat will go with the wind under foresail alone. Give me a chance to get Andreas secure.

Hey, Andreas! You stay there, eh? No wandering. I'm taking you home.

Hopefully won't come to it. I'll let it ride for now. Don't want to deal with all that sail in this wind.

What was that? Wendy's moving. Wendy, you awake?

Wendy: Testing joints in lower limbs. Water penetrating seals. Do you require assistance?

Kit: No. Definitely no. Stay under cover.

Wendy: Balance sensors now attuned. Additional power drain minimal.

Kit: Still no. You're not water…

…

Shit! That's what comes from not looking at the sea. Wave pitched under the stern. Tossed us into the air. Boat came down hard. Damn. Damn and fuck. Andreas is sliding out of the fucking shroud. Stitching's failed.

Andreas! Stay there. I'm coming.

Lashing the tiller. Letting go the halyard. Sails dropping. Come on! Wind's keeping it aloft. Coming down so slowly.

Wendy: Will save Andreas.

Kit: What? No. Go back.

Christ. Got the tiller lashed. Going forward. Boat's pitching. Climbing alongside the cabin roof. Pushing Andreas back into the sailcloth. Teeth marks. Dogs ripped it. Pushing his arm back in. Lashing him down.

Wendy: Rendering assistance.

Kit: No, get back. It's not safe. Get –Wendy!

…

Oh God!

$$\Omega$$

Kit: Wendy is no more. Bows caught in a trough and the boat stopped dead. Threw him off his feet. I was clinging to the cabin roof, lying on top of Andreas. When the boat came up again I saw a flash. That was it. Wendy's gone.

$$\Omega$$

Kit: I've lashed Andreas down. He won't move again. Mainsail's up halfway. That's all I can manage. Taken in the foresail to balance the rig. Boat's manageable, but progress slower. Not all of Wendy is lost. I put a safety wire on him. Attached to his hip. I hauled it in. Batteries must have shorted. Explosion ripped him apart. I have one leg. Shoved it into the cabin. Can you bury a robot?

I'll stick it in Andreas's grave. Serve the bastard right.

Still hoping to make harbour by nightfall. Touch and go.

Transcript 047

Kit: It's the morning of the next day. Weather still rough. Boat's lively and I can hear the anchor chain scraping on the hull. Didn't try mooring last night. Got inside the harbour and dropped anchor fore and aft. Wasn't safe to get alongside the jetty. Made sure the anchors were holding and got some sleep. What a day.

I've told myself since the accident, I can replace Wendy. Got another Wen-Di Helpmate, series whatever-the-fuck-it-is. Another Wendy. Minus the wear and tear of the last fifteen years. Minus the memory, also. The memory I gave him. Years of instruction.

It's not as if I've lost a friend. Or even a pet. It's not that. Yet I mourn him.

Still below in the cabin. Not yet dressed. Now I'm here, the urgency has drained out of me. Don't see how I can bury Andreas where he wanted. Can't physically carry him on my own. Not all the way to that ridge. Just not possible. Maybe he has a cart, or something with wheels. Wheelbarrow I used shifting salt to the jetty is the only thing I recall. And that's too small.

Need to eat something. Can't think straight for hunger. Get ashore. Make a fire. Eat.

Climbing up to the deck. Sun's bright, but the wind's sharp. Should wear something to keep the sun of me. Keep the wind off. Need to bathe. Smell like shit. Smell too much like a corpse.

…

Don't want to remember that. Lying on top of Andreas on the cabin roof…

Too much of a hurry yesterday first thing. Should have guessed the dogs would have had a go at it. Should have checked. Thought of everything that might go wrong with the boat. Never thought about the shroud.

He made it, though. Still tied to the cabin roof. Hole in the shroud. Can see his elbow. Think it's his elbow. Need to fix that.

Boat's a mess. Foresail's trailing in the water. Dropped anchor last night and left everything. Probably didn't even see the sail was in the water. Need to raise sail to get alongside the jetty. Need to get ashore. Fire. Eat something.

Going below. Think there's some biscuits. My stomach's empty. Am I rambling? I think I'm rambling. Need to get myself together.

Wait. There was something last night. Saw a light ashore. So tired I barely registered it, but there was a light near Andreas's house. Think it was a light. Could have been a star I suppose. Just above the horizon. Venus maybe. Maybe the gods of the island are welcoming Andreas back. Seen stranger things.

Apart from that phantom light, nothing's changed…

I take that back. Hadn't seen it because it's the same grey colour as the foreshore. Sailboat, maybe five metres. There's someone ashore. It's their light I saw. Who? Maria Vitalis? Who else could it be? Need to get dressed. Need to eat. Need… everything. Switching you off. Need to get myself together.

Ω

Kit: I'm decent. Well, I'm dressed. Sort of. Still stink. Need to bathe. At least I've pushed all of Andreas inside the shroud. Need to sew it up. Dragged the foresail aboard but something's jammed in the track. Can't haul the sail up the mast. Can't manoeuvre under mainsail alone. Have to swim ashore with a rope. Secure the boat. Then swim back and raise anchor. Wind's onshore so no risk of losing the boat. Apart from the little sailboat, there's no sign of anyone. Surely, if someone were here, they'd have seen my boat.

With any luck, I won't stink so bad after a swim but it will take me a while to get enough rope together. Have to rob most of the running rigging. Not as if I'm in a hurry.

Ω

Kit: Spliced all the rope I can lay hands on and played out sixty feet of anchor chain. Wind's naturally brought me closer to the jetty. Think this length will reach the jetty. If not, I'll have to swim and pull the boat with me. I'll be pulling with the wind so not too bad. Sea's warm. Not too bad. At least I know you're waterproof. Rope round my middle. Here we go. Good to get the weight off my feet. Gentle strokes. Nothing too quick. Beaten up old man. Take it easy. Waves are bigger than I like. Breathing when I can. Rope's dragging behind me. Buoyant. Won't haul me down. Swim. Swimming. Steady. There's someone walking down from the house. So, Mary of life. It's you. Carrying something. Welcome, or warning?

Treading water. See what she wants. Ah. Well, don't blame her. She's got a rifle.

Unidentified human female: Who are you?

Kit: I am Zachariades. Kit Zachariades. You must be Maria Vitalis.

Unidentified human female: I am. Have you seen Andreas Alexandris? He lives here.

Acquiring voice profile.

Kit: I have. He's on my boat. I'm returning him. Can't raise the foresail. Storm damage. May I swim ashore?

Unidentified human female: I cannot see him on the boat.

Kit: He's dead. White thing on the cabin roof is him in a shroud. Promised to bury him here.

Unidentified human female: How do I know you did not kill him?

Kit: Would I bury him if I had? If you use that thing, you'll be the third person to take a shot at me.

Unidentified human female: Zachariades?

Voice profile acquired. Identification Maria Vitalis. Tagged as Maria.

Kit: That's me.

Maria: Andreas told me about you. He said you were a friend.

Kit: That was good of him. He was my friend too. Please. I can't tread water much longer. I don't want to drown.

Maria: Come ashore. But I am watching you.

Kit: I'm not much to look at. But thank you.

Swimming to the jetty. Must explain this thing around my neck before she thinks I'm mad and shoots me. Better. Turning you off for the moment. If you don't hear from me, assume our meeting did not go well.

$$\Omega$$

Kit: Okay, this is recording for the R.H.E.

Maria: Say again.

Kit: Repository of Human Experience.

Maria: I have heard of them. Never met anyone doing it.

Kit: They chose me because of who I was. The last man born.

Maria: Andreas said you were the richest man he had ever known.

Kit: Did he? Doesn't count for anything now. What use is money? There are worse places to be an old man.

Maria: Or an old woman.

Kit: Andreas hated me recording him. You don't mind?

Maria: No. No one will ever hear it. I saw his books were gone.

Kit: He took them with him. Wouldn't part with them. They're all at mine. I came here for salt… I repaired the saltpan. You saw that?

Maria: I saw.

Kit: Found him in a bad way. Drunk. Given up. I thought he'd be better with me. He wasn't well enough to be on his own.

Maria: You do not look so good either.

Kit: Last month has been tough.

Maria: How did he die?

Kit: A stroke. I think it was a stroke. We were harvesting olives. He collapsed or fell. Never regained consciousness. No obvious injury. He told me he wanted to be buried here, up on that ridge. That's why I brought him back.

Maria: He said that?

Kit: Yes. Under a tall pine.

Maria: He told me to bury him behind his house.

Kit: Yeah? Why doesn't that surprise me. If he'd told me that I wouldn't have lost Wendy.

Maria: Who?

Kit: Wendy, my robot helpmate. Andreas didn't like him. I lost him overboard.

Maria: Him?

Kit: The robot. It, him, whatever. Only brought it with me to help carry Andreas to the top of the ridge. Burying Andreas was part of a bargain. If I buried him, I could have this place. It has a saltpan, everything else I need.

Maria: He said that?

Kit: Yes. Looks like we will be neighbours.

Maria: Or rivals. Andreas promised his place to me.

Kit: You think I'm trying to steal it?

Maria: No. I believe you are saying what Andreas told you.

Kit: Then now what?

Maria: You must bury Andreas, or you have nothing. That was your bargain. I made no bargain with him. If you fulfil your bargain then we have equal title.

Kit: And then?

Maria: How should I know? Did he wish us to share? Would that be so bad?

Kit: Last few days have been a mess. Can't think straight.

Maria: How can you think at all while talking into that thing? Is it on all the time?

Kit: No. I can switch it off when I want.

Maria: Then perhaps now you need to think.

Transcript 048

Kit: I don't know what to make of this. I'm alone. Digging a grave for Andreas. Ground's full of stones and I'm at the pick as much as the shovel. Maria Vitalis is away harvesting olives from Andreas's grove. We've agreed that if Andreas said he wanted to be buried on the ridge and also said he wanted to be buried behind his house, then he cannot object if I choose the easier. Besides, I can't physically carry him so far and Maria has no intention of helping.

Did Andreas plan this? I don't mean plan to die, though he must have known it wasn't far off.

Why offer his place to both of us? Because it was in his gift and he could use it for favours? Maybe. He was a cynical old bastard, but never calculating. I keep coming back to the idea he intended us to share. But do I want to share this island? This house? I have a home with everything except a supply of salt. Is that so critical?

At least Maria's company seems more agreeable than his ever was.

Need all my breath. Levering rocks out of the ground, sweat's pouring off me. Hope I don't hit solid rock, but it can't be too far down. A shallow grave, but far enough from the house to be safe. Won't get it finished today, but I don't need to finish today. I'd spend the night on the boat, but it's too miserable. And despite the duralene shroud, Andreas is starting to stink.

I lost Wendy. I fucking lost Wendy and I don't know if it's his fault for lying to me, or my fault for being stupid enough to believe him.

Maria: You are a talker all by yourself. I can see why Andreas did not like you using that recorder. It did not sound like your life story. Just an old man grumbling.

Kit: I talk to myself. Habit. Lived alone for a decade since the ministry evacuated everyone over sixty off my island.

Maria: Too long. May I call you Kit? Zachariades is too long a name.

Kit: May I call you Maria?

Maria: You may. The Vitalis name is scattered. I do not think any of my family are left. You?

Kit: All gone.

Maria: I recall. You never knew your father. That is strange.

Kit: I had an adopted father. He was the only father I needed.

Maria: I meant no offence.

Kit: I took none.

Maria: The ground is bad here. Glad it is you digging and not me.

Kit: Olives aren't easy to harvest.

Maria: No. Not easy. Easier with two. I will make up a bed in the house for you.

Kit: Thank you. I'd sleep on the boat, but –

Maria: Why would you sleep with a corpse?

Kit: I don't want to intrude.

Maria: You are not. Company will be a change. I was beginning to miss Andreas, and then you appeared. I have not spoken to someone who I knew so little about in many years.

Kit: Nor me.

Maria: Well then. Do not be shy. I gave up eating men long ago.

Kit: I haven't spoken to a woman in years.

Maria: We will have to remember what it is to be civilised.

Kit: Yes. And thank you.

Maria: For what?

Kit: Not shooting me when you'd the chance.

Maria: You are recording this?

Kit: Yes. It feels important somehow. It's who we are, what we do. We want someone to listen. We want to pass something on. That's my take on it.

Maria: What was their name again?

Kit: The Repository of Human Experience.

Maria: And we are being human. Yes. I do not mind it so much. But will anyone ever hear it?

Kit: Probably not. Will anyone except us ever know where Andreas is buried?

Maria: No.

Kit: Then does it matter if he's buried at all?

Maria: Yes. It matters. We would know. You would know. You made a promise.

Kit: I've broken promises before.

Maria: You kept this one.

Kit: True. I want to shift that big stone out before I finish tonight. Feel happier then.

Maria: I will make food for us both. You are my guest, until you have buried him. Then you will have earned your place.

Kit: Thank you.

Maria: Do not be long.

Kit: Maria's gone inside. Shall I stay here? Or do I repair the rigging and return to my island? I don't yet know. Had enough of the sea. Weather will only worsen as winter comes in. There are Andreas's olives to harvest and with two of us, the work is halved. I'll not miss Wendy's labour. Nor his company. At least, not so much as I feared.

Perhaps I need not decide until spring.

As for you, I've told you my life story and how I came to my island. There isn't much more to say. I am an old man who talks to himself but no one else need hear it. I need the pickaxe to dislodge this rock from Andreas's grave. Excuse me. I have work to do.

ΣΑΛΤΥΣ Ω SALTUS

Printed in Great Britain
by Amazon